Hard

Cider

Abbey

A barefoot monk mystery

By K.P. CECALA

ISBN-13: 978-1721125746

ISBN-10: 1721125744

Cover art: "Virginia" by Will Harmuth

(from the author's collection)

Brother Odo LeRoi stepped off the Greyhound bus, his sandaled foot hitting the hot, dusty shoulder of West Virginia highway. He stood there a moment, gazing soberly at the bleak scene ahead of him. From the bus driver's radio, a mournful ballad oozed out into the sticky August heat, taunting him:

Got no place to call my own, got no lover, got no home...

He saw a weathered gray shack with broken windows, a lone, rusting, gas pump outside. A tendril of greenery, poison ivy perhaps, crawled from inside the cracked window and wandered up the faded shingles. The surrounding fields rose suddenly and vertiginously from the back door of the shack, as a lone, mangy stray cat struggled to make its way upward.

He threw a questioning look back at the bus driver.

"Monastery's that-a-way..." The driver motioned vaguely toward the west, before snapping the door shut. Odo nodded crisply, to no one in particular, then picked up his single piece of baggage as the bus roared off: A plastic bag, the sort supermarkets sold for 99 cents to promote "green" shopping. He had no idea where it had come from or how it had turned up at his home monastery in Northern Quebec. The bag sported a giant red bell pepper on its side, sliced open to reveal an obscene number of seeds. It contained all his worldly goods: a few ragged white undergarments, woolen socks, rosary beads, his careworn Bible, the Rule of St. Philbert, plus a dozen crisply sharpened pencils, and the thick, tattered, spiral-bound notebook he had to carry around, always, in order to communicate with the world.

Gamely, he began walking west, along the side of the highway. He felt vastly relieved to be off the bus. Already his nausea was fading, and he vowed he would stay put at this new monastery forever, no matter how bad or dirty or heretical it turned out to be; he would never travel anywhere ever again, except on foot.

Three days before, he had left the Abbey of Notre-Dame-de-Glacier in Quebec province, riding with a quarry trucker down to Saguenay; then took a series of buses through Quebec City, Montreal, US Customs in Vermont--where the border guards peered suspiciously at his Canadian passport and birth certificate, but let him pass anyway. After a harrowing transfer at the Port Authority bus terminal in New York City, he managed to find the bus that would take him into West Virginia, deep in the heart of the Appalachian range, where the Philbertine Order's lone American monastery still stood, 127 years after its founding by wandering and seriously disoriented French monastics, who had thought they were still in Maryland.

Now he was here, which seemed nowhere. It was, he thought, as lonely and impoverished as Notre-Dame-de-Glacier, the northern village he had left so far behind. He had reached the hard reality of Skerritville, West Virginia, a town name he had hitherto seen only in fine print, buried in the old, yellowed Philbertine directory of worldwide monasteries. He had somehow imagined a sweet little town of log cabins and clotheslines, nestled in the heart of rolling green hills and wildflowers. But beyond the down-and-out pumping station, he saw only a two-lane road winding up the near-vertical face of a mountain, bordered with weeds and trash; abandoned, slump-roofed barns, and a loudly colored billboard advertising bail-bond services.

He untied and retied his cord, the holy rope about his waist, then started out along the edge of the road, in what he hoped was the direction of the monastery. Short, slight, barely out of his teens, he

4

was nearly completely swallowed up by the full Philbertine habit, a long white woolen tunic and pale-gray-blue scapular—the rectangular, apron-like garment that went over the basic robe, tied with a rope-like cord at the waist. He pulled off his cowl and hood, and stuffed them into his bag. Though quite warm and cozy for Quebec winters, his habit was proving utterly unsuitable for high Appalachian summer. Some passing motorists slowed down to gape at the young, dark-skinned, wooly-haired monk in his bulky robes, hunkering along earnestly with his red-pepper bag swinging, but no one stopped to pick him up or offer assistance. Which was just as well, since Odo would be unable to speak to them: He was, as officially diagnosed by his order, and by the orphanage in which he was raised, a mute. Born, said the brothers and nuns who reared him in Quebec, without a voice.

But he knew that was not quite so. It was a secret he had kept to himself since childhood. He *could* speak. He simply chose *not* to. And since the Philbertines had, at one time, taken vows of silence, it seemed almost natural to the nuns and monks who had raised him. Still, it had been such a long time since he had attempted any kind of verbal utterance, talking felt unnatural to him, a peculiar exercise that actually caused his throat to constrict.

The new monastery, his old abbot had assured him, would understand. He told Odo this just before he himself left for the airport, clutching a briefcase, dressed in his black suit and white collar which made his long gray beard seem grayer and longer. He had been about to fly to Toronto, and then to France, and had just finished explaining to Odo why he could not take him along on his business-class return to the motherhouse in the Pyrenees. "Living on such a flat Canadian tundra for so long, the French mountain air would likely kill you. See, I was born there, so I can take it. But you have an important mission, young Brother Odo. The American abbey, we understand, is in a state of great disarray, falling away from the principals of our great founder. They are profligate and lax. Lazy! Too much concerned with the modern world. You will be their reformer, the revitalizer, you shall show them the way of the perfect monk."

And Odo had nodded, unable to ask Dom Gervaise how he was supposed to do this, if he could not talk, did not understand English very well, and…if the air of the Pyrenees was supposed to be bad for his lungs, would the air of the American Appalachians be any better? He had hundreds of questions, new ones forming constantly in his brain, but had remained silent as usual, obedient to his abbot to the end.

He walked and walked. The Abbey of the Holy Face was supposed to be only a mile or so from the Skerritville bus stop, but the August heat made this stretch of walking seem longer to him than the entire journey from northern Quebec. Sweat poured down his back while the tops of his feet burned in the sandals Dom Gervaise told him to wear. The stiff back strap had scored deep wounds into the backs of his ankles. Yes, it was a great trial, this trip, but he continued on stoically, all in the service of great Saint Philbert.

Yet one more pickup truck whizzed by Odo, sending his robes flying around him and almost knocking the red-pepper bag out of his hand. But he continued on doggedly toward his new home. Not a home, an assignment he would have ever chosen for himself; he'd never had any desire to leave Notre-Dame-de-Glacier or Quebec, never was affected by the wanderlust said to afflict studious students and readers. He'd never had any curiosity about the United States or its culture, though the lights and sheer intensity of New York City and even Cumberland, Maryland, had left him a little dazed, somewhat shaken up. Perhaps, he imagined, like passing through the temporary torments of Purgatory before finally being admitted to Heaven.

He hoped Holy Face Abbey would be a kind of heaven, after this very long trip, although Dom Gervaise had warned him darkly not to expect too much of the American house. Odo really had no idea what kind of conditions were facing him at Holy Face; he could only hope Dom Gervaise was somehow wrong, and maybe it wouldn't be as bad as he feared.

After walking for what seemed miles along the winding asphalt uphill, he stopped at a clearing, where another, thinner, road curved out to meet the highway. There was a signpost, without a sign. He bent down to turn over the wooden slab that had fallen onto the ground: on it, a crudely drawn arrow, *Abbey of the Holy Face, Philbertine Brothers and Fathers*, along with the order's crest and symbol, a hazelnut with a single leaf, set in the center of a cross. This gave Odo some relief; he propped the sign up against the post, then made his way up the thin ribbon of black, a freshly paved road that still smelled of tar. The absolute and perfect matte-black of that asphalt somehow gave him a sense of reassurance, and he began his upward ascent.

This proved a much more pleasant walk, though far more steep. It was utterly silent, but for the call of wild birds, and rustling in the surrounding woods. Dom Gervaise had warned him to watch for snakes; he said America was filled with them. But Odo only saw a peaceful dark path alongside woods that did not seem so different from the woods surrounding Notre-Dame-de-Glacier, heavy with pine, birches and ash. Even though he was sweating more profusely, he felt more at peace now, certain his long journey had not been in vain. He had lost his home, the only one he had ever known, but perhaps the new abbey would seem like home to him sooner rather than later.

At the summit of the hill, he felt puzzled. He had expected, somehow, the monastery would sit at the very top; there was a small clearing there, but nothing else, only a great panoramic view of dramatic green mountains against blue sky, great stratified cliffs stripped of coal and a valley crisscrossed with a busy four-lane freeway, grayish industrial buildings, a truck depot, several trailer parks and, glittering at the far end of the horizon, what looked like a shopping mall, featuring Target's red, bull's eye logo. He felt both relieved and disappointed to see all this: Relieved that the abbey was not, as Notre-Dame had been, literally in the middle of nowhere, many miles from any type of civilization. But he wondered how peaceful the abbey could be, so close to the "world" like this.

But first he had to *find* the abbey. He suspected it was hidden in the woods, but where? Across the clearing, he saw a narrow dirt path leading into the forest, marked with a small, handmade cross nailed to a tree. Ah, he thought. He strode across the field to it, through quivering buttercups and small daisies, blue chicory, a riot of summer flowers. The cross itself seemed the type made of palms, given out before Eastertide, the fronds now faded and ragged at the edges, the artificial orchids set in the center turned gray. He peered into the woods, which seemed as dark as twilight, even though it was the middle of the afternoon. Trust our Lord Savior, he told himself firmly, as he set off down the dark path, hoping the stone walls of the American abbey would soon present themselves to him.

2.

Outside the cider barn at Holy Face Abbey, Brother Emerick Ottlesby set the last half-gallon bottle of Holy Face Hard Cider into the bed of the old pick-up truck, then climbed in himself, claiming the few feet of space before the tailgate. He stretched himself out against a hay-bale set there to steady the bottles, and settled in a for a brief catnap, under the shade of ancient maple. Like most young monks, he had not adjusted to the abbey's 24-hour cycle of liturgy, despite two year's residence already; he still found himself craving a quick doze now and then.

The cider-master was having none of it. "Git your lazy butt into town and deliver that cider!" Brother Isidore snarled, kicking the side of truck for emphasis. Emerick reluctantly sat up. Older than he looked—at 26, he could still pass as a gangly teenager, sandy hair falling across his brow, bright blue eyes, sun-freckles spattered across the bridge of his slightly bumpy nose—the result of a fractious tussle with his older brother at age twelve. His lean, lanky, broad-shouldered physique seemed tailor-made for worn T-shirts and faded denim jeans, but also, paradoxically, the light-indigo-blue scapular and white robe of the Philbertine order, the cotton-linen fabric flowing effortlessly from his shoulders to his feet. His bare feet.

"You skip Vespers again, there'll be hell to pay!" Brother Isidore—the abbey's orchardist and cider-brewer, was a big man, his belly comfortably expanding above his leather work-apron and cord. 'Jolly' was an adjective often used to describe him around the abbey, although Emerick, who was in his employ, knew he had frequent surly moods and a nasty temper. Izzy's round, perpetually red rosacea-ed face was adorned with a comical handlebar mustache, and gay-Nineties sideburns. He grew them that way, he said, to both amuse and annoy his fellow monks. He glanced over the crates neatly arranged in the back of the truck.

"Well, that's the last of it, ain't it, for the season," he told Emerick, in a satisfied way, his words laced with hints of his southern birthplace not too far away, Bristol, the city that straddled Virginia and Tennessee. "Harvest in another month or so. And lo, the cycle of cider begins again."

"Think the new apples will come in okay?" Emerick asked, still sitting in the back of the truck. "With all that junk we sprayed on 'em?"

"Been a damn buggy summer," Isidore growled. "Don't spray no more, we're supposed to be organic. And there's probably some moral issue involved, with mass insect extermination."

"I could ask Lucian about the ethics of it."

"Ah, the hell with that, them bugs gotta go. But we really do need to diversify, 'case harvest really tanks one year."

"Too bad that pale ale thing didn't work out," Emerick mused. "You know, the Trappists over in Siloe are coming out with a porter and some kind of 'winter wheat' ale. Why can't we do that?"

"Because we're not damned Cistercians, that's why. I'm not wasting my time with beer, okay? I got more important fish to fry."

"Oh yeah, your *fah-h-hn lik-kooooor*," Emerick teased, holding an imaginary cordial stem in one hand.

"Go ahead and laugh, farm-boy. You won't be laughing when the money starts pouring into this place from D.C., maybe even New York."

"If money ever does come pouring into this place, I *will* laugh!" He jumped off the tailgate. "Hey, boss, you know what we should do? We should try stilling some actual *moonshine!*"

"Yeah, because that wouldn't be too much of a cliché here in West Virginia, would it."

"It's a *thing!* Even the big bourbon distillers out in Kentucky are doing it."

"Yeah, I'll put you in charge of it, townie."

"Really?"

"No!"

"I was serious, Izzy!"

"Monks making moonshine! New abbot would *love* that!" Izzy snorted. "Well, I think I'm going to stick with my fine lik-kooor. I'll get the recipe straight eventually." The brewer's attempt at liqueur-making had been inspired first by Chartreuse, then by Benedictine, reputedly invented by 16th-century monks and distilled from thirty-one different herbs. Isidore was trying it with forty-one herbs.

"Yeah, but that last batch tasted like foot ointment." Emerick pretended to gag.

"Because you gotta let it sit for a while! A long while! Started this eight years ago, so that first vintage must be near perfection."

"Make Lucian try that. He's the fine spirits connoisseur."

"Did he teach you that word, *connoisseur*?" Izzy snickered. Lucian was the abbey's librarian, a British-born scholar who had come to monasticism relatively late in life after a career as an academic. Emerick scowled at him.

"We talk about things…on a *higher* plane. Spiritual matters. Things I can't learn from the likes of you."

"Lah-di-dah-dah."

"You seen him today? He wasn't at prayers at all today, or Mass. Or at dinner."

"Didn't he leave for France already? Working on that book of his?"

"Maybe. Yeah, I guess that was this week. Didn't even say good-bye." Emerick jumped off the tailgate, a bit mournful. "I'm going now. Gimme the phone, just in case."

"In case what, you want to watch some porn?"

Emerick lunged and snatched the cellphone out of Izzy's hand. He was the only monk who had one; even the abbot used the old-fashioned landline. "In case Maudie tries to renegotiate the price again. I'll call you."

"Just tell Maud she has to pay what everyone else pays for our cider, no special breaks for Mennonites. Or anyone else. And be back before Vespers, or else. No stopping at Dairy Barn for double scoops."

"Hey, if I take my pole and pull some fish out of Stilton Creek…think Brother Cook would fry it up for supper?"

11

"Of course he won't, and you don't got time to go fishing! Just do what you gotta do and get back here!"

Emerick slipped the phone into his hip pocket—pausing first to remove a large, wriggling earthworm: "Guess I don't be needing him." He handed it to his monk-boss with a big grin. Izzy took it, scowling.

"And put some sandals on, you fool. I don't know how you can go 'round with bare feet like that, when the pavement's so hot like now. It just ain't right."

In response, Emerick saluted him and jumped into the driver's seat of the truck. He was the only monk of Holy Face who took the requirement of discalcement seriously, and went about barefoot almost constantly. As a result, his feet had become quite notorious: Yellow-nailed, scarred, deeply dirty, with thick bunions and ugly warts; he was even missing a few toes, which he claimed he'd left behind somewhere in Afghanistan, during his stint in the military. "My soles ain't no reflection on my soul," he'd respond cheerfully, when other monks wrinkled their noses at sight of his feet.

He revved up the engine of the old pickup truck—it had been once, in a former decade, deep oxblood red, but now, dented, rusted at the edges, it had been repainted an ill-advised shade of puce green, which was already beginning to chip off in huge flakes. But it still ran reliably, and bumped along the gravel path off the monastery grounds, the cider bottles tinkling amiably in the back.

The Abbey of the Holy Face had been founded in the 19th century, but had, regrettably, burned down several times since its founding. As a result, the monastery building was now of a 1950s pre-Vatican II vintage, a sober rectangle of local stone and brick jutting out of the hillside, with a starkly plain bell-tower poking into the sky. Its single bell sonorously marked each hour, and the calls for prayer. But the semi-attached chapel was relatively new, built after several bumper apple crops, a soaring timber-framed triangle of river-rock and oak, studded with abstract stained-glass. Just past the monastery proper and the chapel lay the cidery complex, a huge multi-lofted barn which contained the big cider-presses, the bottling machine, rooms filled with empty baskets and crates and apple-picking tools, plus Isidore's "laboratory" and office. Uphill lay the dairy barn, the bee-hives, a fenced-in vegetable garden and the wood-wright shop; beyond, up toward the summit, lay acres and acres of apple trees, summer apples up front, with late-harvest apples nearest the mountaintop. The orchard directly bordered the state or "Heart-break" forest, where drug-overdose victims were sometimes found; but the two areas were kept separate with a tall, barbed-wire-topped fence.

Emerick took the narrow, freshly paved road up over the summit of Stilton Mountain, to get to the Mennonites in the valley beyond. He sang a song of his own invention: Not a Gregorian chant, but something more along the lines of a blue-grass anthem:

I'm goin' to Heaven, yeah I know it well. I'm goin' to Heaven and you're going to—

He suddenly stopped the truck, right in the middle of Stilton Mountain Road. He had just gone past the summit, and now he saw, sitting in the clearing by the side of the road, a monk. Yes, a monk in the distinctive blue and white. But not one of *their* monks. Emerick switched off the truck, leaving it smack in the middle of the road, and waded through the wildflowers to get to him. He stood over him: Emerick was not abnormally tall, but he still cast a long shadow.

"Hey," he said to the little monk who sat crosslegged amid the flowers. The monk looked up at him: Round face, brown skinned, enormous dark eyes with intriguing, thin, bat-wing eyebrows, a full nimbus of reddish-brown hair…He was black, this new monk. No big deal, so was the new abbot. But what was he doing *here?*

"I know who you are. The new guy from Canada. But you weren't due for a few days yet. I'd have met you at the bus stop."

The monk continued to stare up at Emerick. The emotion in his eyes was unmistakable: He was utterly *terrified.*

"Well, whatcha scared of, fella? We're not such a bad bunch! Come on, jump in the truck and come with me. I have a cider delivery to make in town, then I'll take you back and introduce you to everyone…"

Back in the truck, Emerick found himself doing all the talking.

"Maybe they told you before you came? Our industry is apples. We grow 'em, then smash 'em up into cider. Some abbeys do cheese, some do fruitcake, some even do fudge. So I hear. We do apples and cider. Hard cider, for grown-ups, though we do a 'soft' version for kids, too. When the monastery was first founded, they planned to grow filberts, you know, our order's official nut. The motherhouse in France sent over a whole bunch of saplings, but by the time they got there, they were nothin' but kindling wood. So they bought some apples from the Mennonites, saved the seeds and planted those, and they took right away. Of course, they done a lot of work on the orchard since, grafting and new specialty trees and such. Well, Satan tempted Eve with the apple, didn't he, so we play off that a little on our label. Our cider sells out every year; we could make more and be bigger, maybe go regional with it. But that's not really why we're here, just to sell hard cider, is it." He glanced over at Odo, who did not respond, but stared straight ahead, past the crack in the windshield.

"First thing we do, is git you a habit made of cotton. You can't wear that wool down here in West Virginia, you'll die of heatstroke. Save it for winter. We do get some fierce winters on the mountain. But I guess you're used to that and all, being from Canada."

No response. Odo now turned his face toward the window, which he had rolled up tight.

"It's different, I guess, than what you're used to. I mean, I can't imagine, being sent to another monastery. I've *always* been here, 'cept when I was in the Army. I grew up here in Skerritville area, down in

14

the holler, the bottomland just west of town. My brother—my biological brother I mean--still lives there, but Momma lives over in Port Gelding now, at one of those senior-adult condo places. I can imagine it's hard for you, getting sent here. But you'll get used to it." He pulled into a busy parking lot next to a slightly ramshackle log building with a big porch. *Mauds Mennonite Market*, a hand-drawn sign read.

Emerick moved to jump out of the truck. "You coming? It's okay, you can wait here, but it'll get hot in the truck. Maybe you want to stand under that there tree."

But Odo did not move. He did watch as trio of giggly young girls emerged from the store running, barefoot, dressed in colorful calico dresses with black pinafores, their hair braids flying. They ran to the back of the truck, and Emerick greeted them with a big grin. "Hey, sweet things!" he sang, as he filled their arms with half-gallon bottles of cider. He then picked up a big wooden crateful and strode toward the log store with only, Odo noticed, the slightest bit of a limp.

Inside, Maud herself came around the butcher case to meet him. She was a big, solid woman in black and gray, a widow with four girls, her white cap askew over whitening hair.

"Ah, the boy in blue. Praise the Lord, folks been begging for your cider with this hot snap we been having—"

"It's the last we got, Maud, for the season. But the new apples are a-comin'."

"Well thank the Lord again." The Mennonites of Stilton Valley and the monks of Holy Face maintained a mutual respect and affection for each other, despite their dogmatic differences. Maud had been selling the abbey's cider since the very beginning, when old Dom Rasmus and Brother Isidore had revived the old brewery shed nearly a decade before.

Maud's littlest girl, Gracie, ran up to him. "How come you boys wear them blue aprons?"

"Well, darlin', blue is the color of Heaven." Emerick smiled down at her.

"And Emmie's hair!"

Emerick's attention suddenly turned to Maud's oldest daughter, in her late teens, who sat sulking in a corner. She was in flowered calico, but not wearing her white cap, sporting instead a very 21st-century hairstyle, spikily cut and streaked with an arresting shade of blue-purple.

"*Yikes!* Miss Emma, you done got *scalped!*" He assumed a look of mock horror; Emma picked up her white cap from nearby and threw it at him.

Maud sighed, deeply. "Can't hardly control her anymore. Well, she is marrying age."

"Hey Em, what made you go and do a thing like that?"

"What do *you* know about anything?" Emma snarled, snatching her cap back. "Everyone knows, you boys on the mountain *hate* females!"

"Don't show disrespect," Maud barked, but Emerick simply chuckled.

"Not true, Miss Emma! I, for one, sure do like the girls! Just don't have time for one, you know, Brother Isidore keeps me jumping."

"Hear you got a new big boss over there," said Maud.

"Yeah, Dom *Fred-derr-reek.*" He rolled his 'r's in an exaggerated way. "They sent him over from France, just after old Dom Rasmus passed on."

"But he's a man of color, I hear."

"Yeah, he's from Africa originally, one of those French-speaking countries. We're gettin' used to him and he's gettin' used to us. A little rocky but... It'll work out." He gestured toward the truck. "We got a new member, too, a transfer from Canada. A young guy! You know we need more of those, to work in the orchard."

"Why isn't he in here helping you?"

"Well…" Emerick's gaze turned toward the truck, where Odo sat, a stolid, unmoving shadow in the cab. "He seems a mite traumatized, from his trip down here. Not one for words. But we'll take care of him, he'll be fine."

"Sure you will, you're good men, all of you, up there on the mountain. Even if you charge too much for your cider. He's in good hands." She went to her till. "Not going bicker with you today on the price, don't feel like it. Girls, take them crates of damaged vegetables there out to his truck, they're for the monks. Here," She reached under a glass case on the counter, and pulled out a big puffy doughnut, glistening with sugar glaze. "Give this to your friend, the new monk."

Emerick jumped back into the cab, and handed the big doughnut to Odo, who merely gazed at it sadly and turned away. Emerick sighed, then took a big bite out of it himself, as he revved up the engine. He talked, drove and ate the doughnut at the same time.

"Of course she don't have a license to sell liquor. But our cider isn't really liquor, it ain't all that *hard*, it's more like real tangy apple juice. Or lite beer." He licked the glaze off his fingers. "But the authorities don't give her no trouble; they probably buy most of it themselves! Gotta look into that moonshine idea, though they sure won't be able to sell *that*."

Odo said nothing.

"I'm gonna talk to Gary, my older brother, he's the night manager at the Big Roof Inn in Spitztown. And also the bartender. He might…" He glanced over at his passenger, and suddenly fell silent himself. He had a vague sort of feeling, or intuition, that the younger monk was in some kind of great sorrowful distress, the type that usually came with someone's death. The abbot had told them the new member did not or could not speak; they might never know what he was really thinking or feeling. Emerick wiped his right hand on the long skirt of his robe and settled into humming his homemade song, hoping a resolution to the young monk's distress would eventually work its way out.

As they crested Stilton Mountain on the newly paved road, however, Odo jumped, and suddenly shouted: "*Arret!*"

Startled, Emerick brought the truck to a screeching halt.

They were at the very same spot where he had found the young monk, sitting in the meadow clearing. Odo suddenly jumped from the truck, and went running, right back into the woods. Emerick pulled over, jumped out and ran right after him.

"Hey, where you going? Don't go in there! That's not abbey property, it's---"

Only about a hundred yards or so into the woods, Odo stopped short. Emerick barreled into him and nearly knocked him over; he grabbed the young monk's shoulders to steady himself, and gasped, when he saw what Odo had led him to.

At first a flash, of white and blue fabric, like a pile of debris, lying on the forest floor. The Philbertine habit, but this habit still had a monk inside. Emerick now ran to the man on the ground, gently turning him over. It was quite obvious the monk was deceased, though perhaps not for very long.

"*Lucian!*" He gasped, turning pale. For a moment, he seemed unable to speak or form words. Then: "W-why...*How?*"

Odo, now standing beside him, silently looked upwards. Emerick looked, too, and saw, hanging from a tree branch above, part of the monk's white cord hanging down, but snapped and frayed. The other end was wound tightly around Father Lucian's neck.

"No," Emerick whispered, talking to the rope. "No, no, no. Not *possible.*"

Odo motioned toward an overturned stump.

"NO!" Emerick shouted into the woods. But he sank down beside the deceased monk to cradle him in his arms a moment, rubbing the man's arms as if trying to coax him back to life. Then he reached into his own pocket and pulled out the cellphone, hitting a single number.

"Dom Frederíque," he said, in a deeply shaken but calm voice, into the phone. "We found Father Lucian. No, not on monastery grounds. He's on top of Stilton Mountain. In the Heart-break Forest …He's…left us."

3.

Dom Frederíque was not pleased to see all the red and blue lights blinking up on Stilton Mountain Road. He was man of regal height, balding and graying, with long, arched brows, dark copper-brown skin and a faintly dour set to his mouth. He wasn't overly imposing, but somehow the sight of him, briskly walking down the halls of the abbey, with narrowed, questioning eyes behind steel-wire spectacles, stirred up a certain amount of uneasiness among his monks. He now walked over to Emerick, glowering.

"Why do you call the local authorities? This is a monastery matter, *privé* !"

Emerick replied, stone-faced: "Because he was *murdered*, Abbot."

"Uh, don't really think so, Biff." A young woman walked up to them both, short and petite, china-blue eyes, short blond hair cut pertly at her chin. She was wearing law-enforcement blue, her tie perfectly knotted, a gleaming badge on her chest. "And let's face it, this is Heart-break Forest. Everyone in town knows it, and even the monks too—"

"No," Emerick snapped. "Not him, of all people. It's *impossible*, I'm telling you."

"Then tell me more about him," she continued. "How old was he? What did he do at the monastery?"

"Father Lucian Powers," Emerick replied, "was ordained, and originally from England. About 55, he'd been here ten years, I'd reckon. He was our librarian…"

The abbot drew himself up. "Father Lucian was our order's *hagiographer*."

"Whaa-a-a?" she asked, while poking at her computer tablet, "What's that?"

Emerick stepped in. "He studied *saints*. He was writing about our founder."

"Who is this *girl*?" The abbot demanded.

"She's the county sheriff, Abbot. Ardelle Coombs. This is her jurisdiction, since we're outside town. A fellow Army veteran, I might add. Also my third cousin, once removed."

"Biff, I'm sorry," she continued, "but it really looks like…well, suicide. The boys here and I agree. And I seen my share of hangings. Ain't pretty, but this has all the hallmarks. That's why folks come out here, don't they? Give it all up and do themselves in. Usually it's the opioid thing, though. Was he depressed?"

"No! That's the thing of it," Emerick was clearly frustrated. "He wasn't down or gloomy or anything like that. He was a busy man. He was working on a big project, his book on Saint Philbert. He was going to France, to do more research. Come to think of it, his glasses are missing, and his rosary, he always wore those. He was powerful nearsighted, and he always had his beads hanging from his cord—his Sword of Prayer, he called it."

"Glasses and rosary beads…Guess a man don't need neither if he's fixing to kill himself. How well did you really know him, Biff?"

"Why does she call you *Biff*?" the new abbot demanded.

"That was my *secular* name, Dom Frederique." Emerick answered, in a serious way.

"You were *baptized* with that name?"

"No, I was baptized Bramwell Francis Ottlesby Jr. In the chapel of Holy Face, I might add, by a Philbertine priest. 'Twas old Dom Rasmus who give me the name 'Emerick.' Would have chosen something different, if it was up to me." He turned to Ardelle. "I worked with him sometimes in the library. Mostly I was helping him reach stuff on the upper shelves, he had a bad back. But lately, he was also my...*mentor*. Spiritually, I mean. He was showing me the right stuff to read. Aquinas and St. Francis and Benedict. He got me into Saint Thérèse, you know, the Little Flower. He was...*good*. A good man, he took his vows seriously. His vows..." Suddenly Emerick started looking about, as if searching for something.

Odo, who had been standing on the sidelines, seemed to understand instantly. He ran over to the corpse, and picked up part of the cord which had strangled the man, presenting it to Emerick.

"Yep, that's it. Look at it. Only got two knots on it!"

Ardelle and the other officers stared at him in confusion.

"Yeah, so?"

"Philbertine priests, we take *three* vows," said the abbot. "There should be three knots."

"One of the knots is missing!" Emerick exclaimed. "But which one?" He ticked them off on his fingers: "Obedience, stability..."

"Poverty?" Ardelle asked.

"Nah, that's the Franciscans. We are a pretty poor abbey, though."

"With that brand-new chapel y'all got? That must've cost a pretty penny."

"The last knot," the abbot said, drily, "is usually *chastity*."

"No *way!*" Emerick was outraged. "He wasn't interested in....foolin' around! He was *chaste*. Still...the missing knot. It's gotta *mean* something!"

"Oh Biff, you dope, it probably fell off or got untied—"

"These knots don't get *untied*, Dell. It's been cut off!"

21

"Or got pulled off somehow…in the…uh, act." Ardelle gave out an exasperated sigh then looked down sadly at the crumpled monk on the ground. "Coroner should do an autopsy on your friend and maybe that will tell us—"

"No," said the abbot, suddenly.

"Beg pardon?" said Ardelle.

Brother Marion from the infirmary now arrived, carrying one end of a stretcher; his intern, a very young—and very big--Philbertine, in novice whites and bright-red hair, was holding the other. "It's generally not done, with the monks," Marion said now, in a polite way, as they set the stretcher down beside Lucian. "You should know that, Miss Coombs. We usually just have a doctor come up from town and sign the death certificate, and that's that." Marion was a well-groomed man, rimless spectacles perched at the top of his nose, balding with a perfectly trimmed and very short graying beard. "We will bring him back to the abbey, and bury him ourselves, undisturbed. It's part of our Rule," he said almost apologetically.

"But, but—You realize we're on state property, the state forest, don't you?" She looked from the abbot to Emerick, who jumped in:

"Dom Frederique, with all due respect, we need to know if Father Lucian was actually murdered."

"Murdered!" Brother Marion paled. "Gracious, Emerick, how can you *think* that?"

"How is he murdered!" The abbot snapped. "There is rope, there is a man, with deep marks on the neck. There is no one else in sight, no one except—" He now turned to Odo, noticing him for the first time. "This new monk, no? Who does not have the apparent strength to kill a man, I do not think. He is still a *boy*."

Odo winced.

"He had absolutely nothing to do with this," Emerick responded. "He just got off the bus, got lost and stumbled onto this, poor kid. Father Lucian would not have taken his own life! He was against that:

He felt life was sacred. *His* life was sacred. Don't we owe him an investigation?"

Ardelle gave him a sorrowful look. "Biff, to be honest, we really don't have the time or manpower for a murder investigation, and I just don't think...I'm sorry, I don't feel it's warranted in this case. It's an ugly thing, I know. Heck, even good men can lose faith sometimes. Remember that Baptist minister from Twyler who drove his car over the quarry cliff? Turned out he had gambling debts."

"Father Lucian didn't gamble!"

"It is a dark day, a very tragic thing, when an ordained priest takes his own life," said the abbot, more softly now. "Especially to use his own cord. *That* is the sign, I think. Shame. Something brought him shame, something he could not bear...We must accept this hard will of God, because that is what it is, inscrutable as it is to understand. We must pray for him, and bury him, give him peace. But no Mass, and he cannot be buried with the others."

"If he was killed by someone else, then he *deserves* a high funeral Mass and burial in the monk's yard!" Emerick argued. "You're consigning him to Hell, without any kind of trial!"

"Brother Emerick, how many knots are on your cord?"

"One, sir."

"It is for...?"

"Obedience, sir. But—"

The abbot held up a hand, silencing him.

"Well... Don't know what else *we* can do here," said Ardelle, shutting down the tablet she carried. "I'll file my report, but for now we'll just say, unknown causes. I don't want to cause the monastery any additional pain, with news reporters calling and such." She looked at the other officers who had come with her, and they nodded, solemnly.

Emerick gave the abbot a pleading look. "Abbot, can't we please have an official autopsy done? At least to find out if there was a physical reason he *might* have done this. I don't know, cancer, some real bad illness..."

"It does not matter *why*, Brother. The act, it is done. His mortal life, it is ended. If he is innocently killed, then he is in Paradise now, with the Almighty. It does not matter what we do at this point."

"So you guys will take over from here?" The sheriff watched as Marion and his assistant gently picked Lucian up and laid him out on the stretcher. "Watch them raised roots on the path back..." She paused. "Sorry, Biff. I can see he meant a lot to you."

"He was a good man, Dell. A very, very good monk, good and decent and intelligent. But to tell the truth," He gazed after the stretcher, sadly. "I guess I didn't know him as well as I thought I did."

Once the body had been removed and taken back to the abbey, Emerick and Odo remained in the woods. Odo sat on the stump implicated in the hanging, while Emerick searched through the debris on the forest floor, kicking at it with his bare feet, looking for something, anything, to help him understand his mentor's death.

"I know you must think I'm crazy," he said to Odo. "But if you knew Father Lucian, you'd understand. He was brilliant and highly educated, but just a regular old guy sometimes, too. You could *talk* to him; he'd listen and not throw psalms or dogma at you. If I could just find that knot...I don't know why, but I think it would help..." He sighed, then put a hand on Odo's shoulder. "You've had a heckuva day, fella. Arriving here to find a corpse. And a monk-corpse at that. You must have thought you were comin' to the very edge of Hell itself. But we're not such a bad abbey, really. The abbot, he's new and a bit of a hard-ass, but...I think he'll soften up when he gets to know us. But we really need you, our group keeps dwindling, no new recruits...There was fifty of us years ago, now we're down to sixteen, and many near-invalids or worse. You came just in time, to find Father Lucian here. And keep our numbers in place, for now."

Odo gazed up at him. He felt himself beginning to warm to this tall, boyish, barefoot monk, not so very much older than he, who seemed so open and honest and funny, a fellow monk unlike any other he had ever known. Not an ancient over-towering figure or superior, but a potential friend. The abbey of Notre-Dame-de-Glacier had only a half-dozen priests and brothers as he was growing up there, and they all seemed ancient, calcified men; in the end there was only old Dom Gervaise. Now, finally, he would be part of a community, no matter how odd or quirky it was, and that struck him as something faintly miraculous.

"You're happy, ain't you, to be part of a real community again," Emerick said, and Odo was startled to hear him say the very words that expressed so clearly what was in his own head. A coincidence, maybe, or perhaps the desire had been so plain, on his face... He nodded, then plaintively laid a hand on his belly.

"Well, you should've eaten that doughnut! It's okay, almost time for supper, then Compline." He cast one look back at the spot where Father Lucian had been found. "Somehow, though, I'm going to get to the bottom of this, no matter what Abbot or Ardelle says. Poor ol' Father Loo! He can't have done this to himself, he just can't have..."

4.

The Philbertines of Skerritville were poor practitioners in the art of silence, but they did manage to eat their meals without conversation, sometimes with recorded sacred music as accompaniment. But there was no music tonight at supper. Dom Frederique had opened the meal with the news about Father Lucian's passing, putting it in the vaguest terms possible ("Our brother Lucian is no longer with us, but has gone unexpectedly to God"), then briefly introducing the newest monk from Quebec, which made Odo feel like he'd been ordered as a replacement for the monk who died.

But he was grateful for the chance to eat without distracting questions he could not answer. The meal was simple and austere, compared to the heavy, rich food of Quebec: coarse black bread, a cold soup of summer vegetables; some sharp cheese and fresh blueberries and sliced peaches; apparently the West Virginian Philbertines were vegetarians, unlike their northern cousins. Nevertheless, Odo was so hungry he ate double portions, and no one admonished him or even looked askance, as they might have at Notre-Dame-de-Glacier. But he could sense heavy emotion in the air of the refectory, a joint sense of sorrow and puzzlement shared by all the monks at the big table. He glanced over, in a worried way, at Brother Emerick, who sat in a frowning, brooding, way, most of the food on his plate untouched. Then suddenly, Emerick stood up, opening his arms wide.

"Am I *crazy*? No, just tell me. Am I? Am I the only one in this community who thinks Lucian was *murdered*?!

The other monks glanced at him in a startled way, then looked away discreetly, as they did during any dinnertime *faux pas*. All except for one monk, sitting directly across from Emerick:

"Sit down, drama queen." The speaker was a man only a few years older: Brother Callixtus was as tall as Emerick and built in a similar, broad-shouldered way, but the similarity ended there. His longish, dark hair swept dramatically off his forehead, and dark brooding brows shadowed dark gray eyes touched with purplish worry-rings. "Everyone here is affected by this. Not just *you*."

"Well I never would have guessed it, the way y'all are just sitting there, eating like nothing's happened."

"Brother Emerick." The abbot rose, a stern look on his face. "This is not the time, nor the place, for this discussion. Let your brothers *eat*, please. "

"Want to be excused, sir."

"No! Sit down and finish your meal!"

Emerick kept standing for a moment, then hopped back over the bench he was sitting on, picked up his plate and walked into the kitchen. Only Callixtus gasped at this wanton act of defiance. No one dared to look at the abbot.

In the kitchen, Emerick encountered Brother Bartolomeo, or simply 'Bart,' the elderly extern monk, and Brother 'Cook', the kitchen-keeper, whose real name was Joachim de Jesus Espinosa Cortez y Miguel. Between them lay Erdwulf, an ancient sheepdog who had been the beloved pet of the late Dom Rasmus. The dog was underneath the preparation table, eating his own, non-vegetarian supper prepared by the cook, big steaming chunks of beef swimming in a gravy.

"He eats better than we do," Emerick groused. Brother Cook ardently believed that eating was a dangerous kind of sensual pleasure, and so took steps to ensure his meals were especially palate-dulling. In his eyes, enjoying one's food too much was like a breach of chastity.

"What's the matter, boy?" Bart asked him. "We heard you raisin' a holy ruckus out there." Brother Bart was a fellow West Virginian, from the coal town of Zero Mines, some thirty miles south of Skerritville. He had been in the monastery for over seventy years, having entered as a teenager. Emerick's family had come originally from those same mine-lands, where his German and Welsh ancestors had worked themselves underground into early graves, so it was possible he and Bart were related. Though hunched over with age, his hair and beard white as snow, the extern monk was still alert and spry, continuing to perform his duties as gatekeeper, head of reception and visitor services.

"I'm with you, Biffie," he said now. " 'Tweren't no suicide. Lucian was too smart for that."

Brother Cook nodded somberly in agreement. "The man Lucian…he do not eat like the man in despair." Joachim did not dine with the brother monks he cooked for, remaining in the kitchen and covertly observing them, other times sitting by the kitchen door to stare off into space. Lucian had suggested he might be a mystic, but no one knew for sure. He was somewhat humorless, with a terse way of talking, black beard and long inky hair which hung past his shoulders, making him look like a dark, greeting-card Jesus. He had recently taken, however, to wearing his long hair in a sumo-style man-bun atop his head, after the monks complained about long black strands turning up in stews and casseroles. Reputedly he had been a guerrilla fighter somewhere in Central or South America—or, more likely, a cook for a guerrilla army. Like Emerick, he eschewed shoes, but kept his own feet wrapped up in beige Ace bandages, to protect them from dropped glasses and dollops of boiling oil.

Emerick leaned forward. "He did not eat like a—what do you mean by that, Chef?"

"He ate *well*. Too well. He enjoyed his food muchly. The man in despair, he does not eat so good." He looked, meaningfully, at Emerick's nearly full plate.

"Thanks, guys," Emerick told them both. "The abbot and the others, they think I'm loony. But I know I'm not imagining it."

The cook peered into the refectory. "The new little one…he do not eat like a man wanting death, either."

"At least someone likes your cooking."

"He is from Brazil, no? Caribbean?"

"Northern Canada, actually."

Cook's face fell into a look of stern confusion.

Bart handed Emerick a leash. "Here, why dontcha take Erdie out to his new bed in the cider barn?" The abbot had banished the dog from its night-time lair in the visitor's parlor.

"Well sure." Emerick knelt to nuzzle the dog affectionately. "Mean ol' abbot, making you sleep in the barn."

"He can't help it, he's allergic. Say, Momma and Gramma coming by next weekend?" Bart asked, hopefully.

"I expect so. Be sure to come round and say hey." Emerick picked up the dog's leash, coaxing him to his feet.

"I'll set the lawn chairs out for y'all." Bart called after him, as he took off with the dog.

Only a moment later, Odo meekly entered the kitchen with his empty plate and placed it in the sink. He looked dolefully at the two monks.

"Something you are wanting, small one?" Cook asked him, brusquely.

"Mmmm-rick?" Odo asked, tentatively.

"He just went over to the cider barn, to tuck in old Erdwulf," said Bart, adding in a warning voice, "But don't be following 'round after him, like a puppy, Abbot won't like it. You got to like all the brothers equal-like."

Odo nevertheless left through the kitchen door, making his way to the barn just uphill from the monastery. He paused at the doorway, watching as Emerick helped the old dog into a shallow wooden box lined with soft old clothes and quilting, then gently massaged its back, humming some odd little tune. A dog lullaby, perhaps, as Erdwulf's eyes closed contentedly. Emerick glanced up at Odo.

"Poor Erdie, kicked out of the abbey. Lucian *loved* this guy. Claimed he was part Irish wolfhound, but don't know about that. Used to take him up to the hermitage, to keep him company while he prayed." Emerick smiled ruefully. "Got to love him twice as much now that Lucian's gone." He let Odo come over and tentatively stroke the dog's head. "A little nervous with dogs, are you? It's okay," Emerick told him. "I think he'll take to you real quick."

At Compline, the two young monks sat together somberly. The monks had assigned seats—stalls, actually, as in most monastic chapels, which sat on either side of the altar. But the stall next to Emerick's was empty, its assigned inhabitant languishing in the infirmary more or less permanently now. Odo nestled in beside him and Emerick silently showed Odo where the prayer books were stowed, then opened his book to the proper psalm for him, and Odo felt grateful.

This abbey was so very different from Notre-Dame, and the chapel here was no exception. Rather than the dusty fussy Gothic edifice Odo was used to, the timber-framed Chapel of the Holy Virgin of the Mountain, with its soaring ceiling and generous slab altar, had been constructed of native stone and wood from the nearby forests, slate and granite, chestnut, oak and ash. Inside, a large portrait of the Virgin with her Child had been painted, he thought, to resemble a Native American woman, with long black braids, dark-earth eyes and deeply tanned skin, baby Jesus in her arms but in a papoose. A single, splendid stained-glass window rose over the side end of the slate-stone altar, an abstract creation of many colors, which seemed to him birds, doves and parrots perhaps, flying up to heaven. The window delighted him, and filled him with a kind of joy; he felt the sense a new phase of his life was beginning, a new, different road into his future. He was nearly overwhelmed by the sound of male voices, the voices of simple men and workers, rising *a capella* in song, rising up, with the glass doves, into the heavens above.

He glanced at Emerick, who sang softly—and off-key--under his breath, but saw his bare, mud-caked foot tapping the stone floor as if with impatience. Odo sensed his urgency, his desire to go out and look for some kind of truth. Odo, too, was beginning to believe the monk Lucian had been killed. Why would a member of this sweetly peaceful community, who apparently lived only to praise God, grow apples and make cider, want to leave it and the earth is such a harsh, shameful way?

Brother Emerick slipped away as quickly as he could at the close of Compline, making his way to the opposite end of the monastery, where the library was. He sensed he was being followed, so he turned, and saw the new monk shyly following. He motioned for Odo to join him.

In the library, Emerick snapped on the light and took a seat behind the desk, setting his hands palms-down on top of it. It was a modern sort of library, with blond-wood shelves that only ran halfway up the walls, which were covered in modern religious art: Wood-cuts, mosaics and abstract paintings in vivid colors.

"Wish I knew what I was looking for," he muttered. "But this is where Lucian worked. There must be some kind of clue, a note, something...." He shuffled through some of the papers on top of the desk: letters to other abbeys, invoices, cards for books that had been checked out by the other monks. He picked up what seemed to be a print-out of an airline ticket--round trip from Washington, D.C., to Paris, France—and regarded it sadly.

"It's for... *tonight*," he murmured. "He was just about to leave on that big trip to finish researching Saint Philbert. See why this all doesn't make sense?"

Odo nodded.

Emerick glanced at the desk calendar, opened to yesterday's date. He flipped a page. "Hmm. Don't say here, *good day to die*." He flipped back a few pages. "Mostly empty. Here, on August 2...Just says, *Mary*." He frowned. "Is that our Lady? Or just some woman named Mary? Well, he was very *Marian*. Unlike me. I always have trouble with that; maybe 'cause my own momma's meaner than a rabid bat. What's that? Look *in* the desk? Well of course I was going to." He tugged at the drawers, all of them. "Locked up, dammit, what was he hiding in here? Key, key...." He ran his hands along the surface of the desk. "Must have been on him. They're prepping his body now; let me go down and see if they found it in his habit. I want to talk to Brother Marion anyway, he's our infirmarian and undertaker, all in one. He's got a keen eye, and notices things. I'm sure he'll do a kind of autopsy himself." He paused, at the doorway, as Odo moved to follow him out. "I better go down there alone. You stay here, and look for stuff. Clues. Anything you think might be of interest."

As soon as he left, Odo went and sat behind the big desk. He studied the keyhole in the center drawer for a while, then picked up a small pair of scissors from a jar in the corner of the desk. He opened them, then inserted the tip of one blade into the keyhole lock. He turned it one way, and then another, and after about fifteen minutes or so, the drawer popped open.

He had never seen a crime or mystery show on TV. He had never actually *watched* television: No cable or satellite dish had ever reached the icy plain of the monastery up north. But he had learned the trick one day when Dom Gervaise accidentally locked them both out of the abbey on a sub-zero Christmas night after Mass in the chapel across the fields. He began shuffling through the contents of the desk. Father Lucian, it seemed, was a very tidy man. The top drawer only contained pens, pencil, and a single book of matches, from a steakhouse in Skerritville. In the drawers, he found empty folders, blank stationary, an old typewriter ribbon, faded with age, though, strangely, there was no typewriter. One drawer contained only index cards, in various sizes, and bottles of mucilage. But in a deep bottom drawer, there was something of interest.

He pulled out a book. A large, leather-bound book, perhaps from the turn of the century. It seemed to be some kind of botanical treatise, and he flipped through page after page of lovely watercolor plants and leaves and trees. But he couldn't read it, because the text was in Chinese. About a quarter of the way through, he saw that a page had been ripped out, leaving a ragged trail of paper running along the inside gutter of the book.

"Not the best way to start your first day at Holy Face Abbey," a sharp, but deeply male voice rang out. Odo looked up and saw the dark-haired monk who had rebuked Emerick in the refectory. "Breaking into the librarian's desk, are we? What kind of little thug have they sent us from Quebec?"

Odo could only stare at him.

"Ah yes, you're mute, the abbot says. It doesn't matter. All you need to do is listen. To *me*."

Odo moved to pull his notebook and a pencil from his chest-flap pocket, but the monk laid a steely hand on his wrist and pulled him up out of the chair behind the desk. "Allow me to introduce myself. I am Brother Callixtus, the new librarian and also... Master of Novices. And you are to consider yourself a novice, for the next six months, until we judge whether you are worthy of remaining in our community. I will show you your room, and explain to you your responsibilities, which will be exceedingly humble to begin with. You will not be working here, nor with Brother Emerick, but early mornings in the dairy barn, with the cows; afternoons with Brother Cook, in the kitchen. I will meet with you one hour a day, after dinner, for spiritual instruction. Is that clear?"

Odo nodded obediently, but felt deeply disturbed, by the lack of charity he heard in the man's voice.

"And another thing," said the monk, as he led Odo down the darkened corridor to his assigned room. "You will refrain from following Brother Emerick around like an acolyte. I understand: Like a baby bird imprinting on the first human it sees, you have accordingly become irrationally attached to him. But he is a poor excuse for a monk, and sets a bad example for novices in general. I don't know what kind of perversions you Quebec brothers indulged in, but here he is only a fellow monk, and you will regard him as you regard all the other members of this community. If you are in need of a mentor...*I* will serve in that capacity." He stopped in the middle of the hallway. "Do I make myself clear?"

Odo nodded, mournfully. At Compline, he had been exulting at his good fortune, to be set among a warm and welcoming community, but now found the light had dimmed a bit. He glanced back down the hall toward the library, grateful that he had, at least, been able to leave the Chinese botany book open to the missing page, hopefully for Emerick to discover later.

5.

In a wing off the back of the abbey, the infirmarian Brother Marion was preparing the body of the deceased for burial, washing it, then dressing the corpse in a simple cotton shroud. Philbertine habits were too valuable to be buried, and would be passed on to a living monk of similar size to the deceased. The body would be wound in a linen cloth and buried in a plain white-pine box, one that had been constructed on site by the wood-wright Brother Damascene. But the abbot had already decreed that Lucian could not buried in the consecrated monk's yard alongside the others who had gone before him: Because as a suicide, he was assumed not to have died in a state of grace.

Marion was a calm and reasonable sort of man, undisturbed by the presence of death, no matter how grim or grotesque; a trained nurse and emergency medical technician, the infirmary was his responsibility. Here he had five mostly elderly and bedridden monks in his care, in various stages of vegetation; they occupied single rooms just down the hallway, and an occasional cry or yelp could be heard from that direction.

Marion greeted Emerick with a crisp nod, and invited him, with a wave, to join him at the table, where Lucian's body now lay, in a thin plain gown of white.

"I've been half-expecting you," he said, quietly. "You seem calmer now…Are you coming to accept this?"

Emerick studied his mentor on the table for a moment: Washed up, stretched out, he looked more now like the live man Emerick remembered, handsome, dignified, white haired, deep-set eye sockets, which had contained the wisest eyes, Emerick thought, that anyone ever had: A curious mix of brown and moss green, eyes which seemed to see everything from behind his mock-horn-rimmed spectacles, taking in the world in an amused, but serene sort of way. Those eyes had an amazing way of fastening onto your face, as if he were using them to listen, instead of his ears.

And he always listened, no matter how stupid or ignorant one's words might be. When he spoke, you *had* to listen, for his voice was deep, warm. Even laced with that British accent, it was always as bracing as warm broth on a frigid winter day. He'd been startled once, when Emerick had remarked on his 'high-class' accent; raised in an orphanage in Yorkshire, he told Emerick he actually had a northern, working-class inflection most Brits would not find edifying.

"You and Bartolomeo have the best English dialect in this abbey," he had told Emerick, "a true working-man's American, honed by centuries of history, filled with the echoes of the mountains and the depths of the coal mines." Emerick had been mightily pleased by that.

And he pondered now, the one, potent, bit of advice Lucian had given him.

Be still and know that I am.

Lucian had told him that: The word of the Lord, advice from above. *You are always running about, always here and then there, always talking or fidgeting or humming, you need to be still, boy! Be still and await your instructions; how else are you to learn what the Lord has planned for you?*

Only a week ago, he had spoken with Lucian at length, sitting beside him behind his big desk in the library. He confessed to Lucian that he could not stop thinking about leaving the abbey. He was just still so unsure, if it were the right place for him to be. *You're not ready yet for that decision,* Lucian had told him. *This is your period of discernment. Give it more time. You've grown so since you came here, my son, you are so much wiser and calmer and steady. Your vocation will find you here, it may come when you least expect it.*

"I understand you found him, you and the new arrival," said Marion. "In the woods, where the locals reportedly go…to die?" Seeing the stony expression on Emerick's face, Marion went on: "It's not such an outrageous concept, only here in the US. In Japan, they have suicide forests, and in other countries the dead are laid out in nature…"

"Lucian didn't die a natural death," Emerick snapped.

"Who is to say, suicide is not natural?"

"*We* are! Our Church forbids it!"

"A rule that we should question, don't you think? It was created at a time when men did not fully understand how their minds and bodies and psyches worked—"

"With all due respect, I don't want to have a theological discussion with you right now, Brother Marion. I want to know exactly *how* Father Lucian died. Don't hold back on the details. I can take it."

In response, Marion, pulled aside Lucian's cowl, pointing to still raw, purplish marks stark against the dead man's sallow neck. "Hanging is a brutal, but swift way to die. Asphyxiation, and indeed, his neck is broken…Yet, I don't believe he suffered. He probably had a very *calm* death."

"How can you say that, for sure?"

Marion paused. "Lucian had arthritis, in his hip joint. Very painful. He was taking painkillers, under my care—"

"Oxycodone? Percocet?"

"Yes, you certainly know all about those, Brother, don't you? So you know, they're powerful and effective opioids."

"What half of Skerritville is strung out on..."

"Alas, yes. But these drugs have their uses. Father Lucian was taking a highly controlled amount, but he might have been saving the pills I gave him, one at a time, then took them all at once---"

"Just before he hung himself?"

"Perhaps...A toxicology report would prove that, but of course the abbot has forbidden it. I have another theory, too. If Father were trying to wean himself off the medicine—which he indicated once, he wanted to do—he may have developed suicidal tendencies along with withdrawal—"

"I didn't have that. When I...I mean, withdrawal was sheer hell, and it took months but...I never got so low I wanted to off myself."

"Everyone is different, Emerick. Not everyone is *you.*"

"Well, where's his glasses, then? He always wore them. And his rosary."

"I can understand why he took off the rosary. The glasses...well, perhaps it was like the way some people blindfold themselves, before doing this sort of thing."

"It makes no sense to me that he would kill himself. He wasn't *depressed.*"

Marion looked Emerick in the eye. "Why *don't* you think Lucian committed suicide?"

" 'Cause I just don't."

"Hillbilly wisdom, eh? Sorry—" he said, when he saw Emerick's face tighten. "But it's just so obvious to me."

"Look at that expression on his face. It's *peaceful.* Is that the face of a man who died by...by... asphyxiation?"

"That's why I think drugs were involved. Also what you're seeing is…likely, *relief.* A release, from his earthly pain. You knew he had cancer, several years ago?"

"Yes. Prostate." Emerick shuddered. "But he beat it, he said."

"Perhaps. I suspect it might have metastasized. He may have been terminally ill."

"But you would know that for sure, wouldn't you? Aren't you supposed to be taking care of us?"

"I made a referral to a specialist in town for a check up, not long ago. He refused to go."

"Even so…" Emerick said, slowly. "I don't think he would have chosen to do himself in. He would have stuck it out to the very end."

"I understand your difficulty in accepting this. I didn't know Lucian *that* well. But I admit, he didn't seem like the type to choose this particular way out. He had a wonderful reputation here, everyone liked him, and respected him. He was working on a massive and important project. But we don't always know what's in a man's head, or heart."

"But there's the thing about his knot. You know, the third knot?"

Now Marion, somewhat surprised, walked over to another table, where Lucian's habit sat, folded, the frayed cord on top. He picked up a piece of it. "Yes, that *is* odd, isn't it? It does seem to have been cut off, intentionally." He gazed up at Emerick. "Perhaps… that was his suicide note."

"What, you mean a message? He was trying to tell us something by chopping off his own knot?"

"Certainly. Father was very literary, he loved metaphors and poetry and cutting his cord may have been a way of…symbolically withdrawing from the community, cutting himself off from us."

"If he were depressed enough to commit suicide, he wouldn't be thinking about leaving hints and clues for us, Marion. Someone else snipped it off. I don't know, maybe as a souvenir, or proof that they killed a monk, someone sick…High on drugs, maybe. Someone maybe trying to smear him, ruin his reputation—"

"You're not suggesting a fellow Philbertine, I hope!"

"Of course not. Who here would be capable of doing something like that?"

"Well…You'd be one of the few around here strong and healthy enough to string him up. And you always seem to be disappearing, at odd times." He chuckled at the shocked look on Emerick's face. "I'm *teasing* you, Brother. It could easily be our hefty new novice as well, couldn't it?"

"Not funny, Marion. I'm serious about this!"

"I know you are, but you're letting grief and sorrow cloud your thinking. I think the whole idea of Lucian taking his own life is so distressing and unexpected that you want someone to blame, you want to believe he was killed. But why would someone do that, Emerick? There is no motive, no reason to kill a poor, bookish monk, is there?"

"I guess I should forget about that knot. Maybe it's a red herring… To throw us off the trail."

"Shall we start calling you Father Brown now? Monk-detective?"

"Please don't make fun, Marion." He looked up and now saw Brother Christoph, the hulking novice, standing by the door, regarding both him and Marion with a vaguely hostile expression. Christoph had only joined the order about six months before, a local boy whose family Emerick did not know. He was eighteen, just graduated from Skerritville High School, and he was as tall as Emerick himself, with vacant gray-brown eyes and an uncombed mop of reddish hair. A true cipher: His vocation did not seem immediately apparent, but Marion had been singing his praises as a "huge" help with the infirm monks.

"Anything else, Brother Marion?" the boy asked.

"Not now, Chris, go and attend to your studies." He glanced at Emerick, his eyebrows raised in slight skepticism. "He's studying for Holy Orders. Wants to be a priest."

Emerick looked back wistfully at the boy's departing form. "Well, good for him, if he's got the Call." He gazed back down at the monk lying on his back, still looking innocent and peaceful; Marion had arranged his arms in an X across his chest.

"I'm going to get to the bottom of this, Marion. Something is very wrong here, and I aim to find out that it is."

"Well, then think about this, Brother: Before you accuse anyone, or try to canonize Lucian as an official Philbertine martyr and saint, perhaps you should try playing the role of *Advocatus diaboli.*"

"Yeah, I know what that is, but—"

"No, you need to think about it. If you're going to cast him as a victim, then find out *why* he would be one. Look more deeply into Lucian's life. You might learn something you don't want to know about him."

"You say that like you know something about him."

"I don't," Marion said, blandly. "But I would be curious to see what you come up with."

"I don't need to investigate my mentor. But I will find out why he was killed."

In response, Marion silently and reverently lifted an edge of the linen winding cloth, and laid it over the deceased, hiding his face from view.

The ceremony for Lucian was a simple affair, the briefest of Masses with no music or singing, only a short, dignified homily by Dom Frederique recognizing the priest's work and lamenting that his much anticipated biography of St. Philbert would likely never be finished. The rough pine box-casket was not brought all the way to the altar, as it might be with monks supposed to have died in grace; it was left in the aisle by the door, while the other monks stood stoically beside it.

Brother Callixtus, the new librarian, was the only monk who openly wept: He did so quietly and almost inconspicuously, tears rolling down his composed face. Odo, surprised by this show of emotion, nudged Emerick, who nodded. "Yeah, they worked close together," he whispered. "Guess ol' Clix is human, after all."

He then stepped forward with Christoph—since they were the only two brothers with any real brute strength—to pick up the coffin, heaving it up onto their shoulders and moving out of the chapel with it. Led by the abbot, they carried their brother Lucian past the monk's graveyard, and out past the gates, to an empty field just beyond the boundary of the monastery, where a hole had already been freshly dug, nearly six feet deep.

Brother Emerick himself climbed down into the hole along with Brother Christoph to help steady and lower the box into place, just as a grayish dawn was breaking against the line of eastern hills. Emerick wore shoes today, or more precisely, a newish pair of white Converse high-tops. He glanced down at them, then up at his fellow monks.

"Out of respect. He would have wanted me to be *calced*, for this."

He bent low over the coffin once it was settled into place, placing his hand on its wooden surface. "Promise, Father Loo, I'll figure this out, somehow," he whispered. Odo, standing close by, wondered if he were the only monk who had heard.

Emerick then climbed up out of the grave, picked up a spade, and helped Christoph swiftly cover the coffin with the pebbly reddish dirt piled nearby. Some of the monks began to wander back toward the abbey, as a slight rain began to fall. Callixtus, overcome with grief, had not even made it to the gravesite. But Odo stood and watched as the two young monks finished burying Father Lucian. He felt bad for Emerick, who looked more downcast than ever, as he

41

grimly, almost angrily shoveled spade after spade full of dirt onto the remains of his mentor. Odo went to take a step toward him, but suddenly felt the abbot's firm hand on his back, pushing him toward the monastery kitchen and his new chores there.

In the kitchen he was greeted by somber, silent Brother Cook, who simply handed him a large sack of potatoes, and a peeler. There seemed a faint hostility in this gesture. Odo went and sat on a stool just outside the kitchen door and thoughtfully peeled off long spirals of potato skins, wondering over the mystery of a death, the death of a man he had never even known.

Emerick went back to the chapel, his habit streaked and dusty with reddish grave-dirt, and now sat alone in his side stall, facing the altar. He didn't like how he felt, all hot and angry and prickly and agitated. He wanted to just jump up and run off somewhere, but instead he forced himself to try and just sit still, trying to quiet his brain. *Be still and know that I am...* "I know, *I know...!*" he murmured, as if arguing with an imaginary opponent, shutting his eyes tightly, putting his hands to his face. He put his hands down, and tried to breathe, in the way the therapist had taught him, in the VA hospital. Deep breath in, hold it, one...two...three...four...five... After several of these he felt a little calmer, so he continued, sitting alone in the darkened chapel, simply breathing, and chanting in his head: Be still and know...Be still. Be still.

And a few hours later, when the other monks filed in for Terce, they found him still sitting here, his head bowed and hands folded together, gently snoring and peacefully asleep

.

6.

Odo struggled to make himself useful to Brother Cook in the kitchen, but it felt like a losing battle. He peeled the potatoes, but

Cook told him his peels were too thick; he tried to fill the cookpot with water but ended up dropping it on the floor, denting it and causing a minor flood; he accidentally tipped over an open container of flour. All the while, the usually silent Cook unleashed a torrent of angry Spanish at him, which Odo guessed contained some untranslatable obscenities.

When he and the cook were standing at the table in the center of the kitchen, plucking the stems and strings off the garden green beans, Brother Cook confronted him:

"Why do you not *talk*!"

Odo looked up at him. Did he really expect a spoken answer to that question?

"I tell you why," Cook continued, picking up a paring knife and waving it about in a threatening way. "Some will say, you are full of trauma. A bad event, or person, has steal your voice. Psychological." He pronounced the word *sick-oh-log-ical*. "But everyone have trauma. I have *mucho* trauma! Brother Emerico and the cider-monk, the soldiers, they have trauma, see ultimate evil, and yet they speak! Emerico, too much! But you, little one, I do not believe you have such trauma."

Odo did not look up at him or respond in any way; he focused on the bean he was de-stringing.

"This is what I think. You do not talk...because you are *rebel*!"

Now Odo's head shot up, and he looked at Cook with renewed interest.

"Yes, this is so! You rebel against your superiors and authorities, with silence! It is your way, to take stand, to...to be a man, against the evil and injustice of the world! It is most interesting, I think. It takes courage, it takes a strongness...not to give in, and babble, like an idiot."

Odo considered this. It was not a thought that had ever crossed his mind before, and perhaps wasn't quite true, but now that he had heard this theory, he liked it. And so when Cook suddenly ordered him to drop what he was doing, and set out the dishes for dinner, Odo pleasantly ignored him and silently continued his work with the green beans. But Brother Cook grabbed the bowl of beans from him, and roughly pushed him into the refectory.

"No rebels in kitchen!" he shouted.

Just a day after Father Lucian's burial, Emerick donned his work-tunic and worn apron; but made his way to the library. There was little to do at the cidery today, little to do until the apples really started coming in; he thought Brother Isidore wouldn't mind letting him take a little time off.

He snapped on the light in the library, relieved not to see Brother Callixtus, the translator and new librarian, there. For just a moment, he expected to see Lucian himself behind the desk, his glasses slipping down his nose, his head resting in his hand as he studied some volume or paper. Sometimes he napped in this position, snoring a bit loudly; Emerick had taken to carrying a goose-feather in his pocket, to poke into his nostril. He went to the unmanned desk now, and to his surprise, saw one of the desk drawers ajar.

"Why that little devil…" he murmured, with a grin. "How'd *he* get it open?"

He began checking out the contents of the desk, drawer by drawer. But his attention was caught by the book that still lay open, on top of the desk. He saw immediately, where the page had been torn out.

"That's…weird," he muttered, not immediately seeing any significance in what seemed a senseless bit of vandalism. But thinking better of it, he turned to the back of the book. The book was, of course, in Chinese. But there was, as he'd hoped, an index of Latin plant names, with their corresponding pages in Arabic numbers.

The missing page—34—had been a depiction of a plant called *Panax Emericus*. Emerick was startled to see himself linked to the plant through his Philbertine name. He remembered old abbot Rasmus giving him that name when he entered Holy Face as a novice. Saint Emerick had been a medieval prince, the son of the king and saint Stephen of Hungary. It was also the English version of the baptismal name of the mapmaker Amerigo Vespucci. "Basically," the old abbot said, with a smile, "You are 'The American.' And you certainly are the most American monk, I think, we have here, considering your time in the armed forces, defending our country."

He'd have to find out what *Panax* meant. Somehow he sensed it had little to do with *pax*, or peace. He rummaged about in the top drawer a little more, and way toward the back, his fingers stumbled upon the cold steel of a key. Not the key to the desk, he thought, but likely to a particular structure on monastery grounds. Now Emerick rose, the silver key clutched tightly in his palm, and walked the length of the long narrow library, to a window that overlooked the barnyard, orchards and ascent up to the mountain's summit.

Several hundred yards into the woods, near the mountain top, lay the monastery's hermitage. It was a controversial sort of structure, erected in the 1980s by an abbot who wholeheartedly supported solitary prayer and reflection as a route to God. But it was also a troublesome place where wayward monks could get themselves in trouble. After reports of drunken parties and even a brawl, it was shut down for a while and several brothers were dismissed; then Abbot Rasmus had allowed limited access to a few select monks of proven piety, such as Lucian. But even then, only for a day visit, or an afternoon; overnights were strictly forbidden. Even to walk up to it required permission from the abbot.

If he watched the time, Emerick thought, he could hike up there and back before Terce and dinner. No use, he thought, in asking permission from the abbot. He had heard the new abbot did not approve of the idea of the hermitage at all, asserting Philbertines were meant to live actively in community, not in hermetic solitude and silent contemplation. Well, he would just take a little hike in that direction. Maybe see if the key actually fit in the door there…

On his stool outside the kitchen, Odo set down the turnips he was peeling, and put a small crust of bread he had saved from breakfast in the palm of his hand. He held his hand out hopefully, and soon, a tiny, brilliantly colored bird came, perched confidently on his finger, and choked down the little treat. Odo cupped his hands gently about the bird, not daring to breath, admiring its beautiful feathers and delicate features.

As a little boy growing up in the northern Philbertine abbey, he had learned this trick; the birds of northern Quebec were drabber and grayer, though no less fascinating. One day—perhaps he was six, or seven--he closed his fist around one in delight, intending to bring it back to his room as a pet. He held it tightly as he walked back to the abbey, but when he arrived, found that the bird's life had been extinguished in his own small hand.

He opened his hands now and the bird flew off; he watched its flight through the sultry, buzzing air. He picked up his peeler and the turnip he had been working on, and resumed his chore.

"Hey, put that vegetable down," Emerick called out cheerfully. "Come take a walk with me."

Odo froze and glanced back into the kitchen. Emerick continued: "It's all right, we won't be gone long. Hey Cook!" he yelled into the kitchen door. "Gonna borrow this guy Odo for a few minutes!" Then to Odo: "You're not afraid of him, are you? Brother Cook *is* scary-looking. But harmless."

In response, Odo pulled out his notebook and pencil and began printing out the name CALLIXTUS in big block letters. Emerick laughed out loud.

"Oh, don't worry about *him*, neither. He's what I'd call..." He leaned over, in a conspiratorial way. "A *re-enactor* monk. You know how guys re-enact the Civil War, dressing up and acting like Confederate generals? Clix is from California, near Hollywood, a failed actor I think. He is very *dramatic*, but it's all an act. Sometimes he plays the Spiritually Tortured Monk, but mostly he enjoys being Inquisition Monk, like that Savonarola guy. But he's got no real control over anyone. There is no official novice-master anymore, because except for Brother Christoph in the infirmary, we have no novices. You're a grown man, and a brother in full, you don't have to take no nonsense from him. C'mon, let's hike up the mountain a bit. I'm going to show you the hermitage."

They stopped by the barn to pick up Erdwulf, adjusting their own pace to accommodate the dog's aging gait.

"That arthritis is really slowing him down," said Emerick, softly. "I hear there's doggie pain pills for it, I'll have to see if maybe Marion can get some, although he'll probably get all biggety and say Erdie doesn't count as a brother-monk."

The hermitage hut was not quite what Odo expected: He had envisioned a tiny cabin hewn from logs with a stone chimney, furnished only with a hard wooden platform for sleeping. But the 'hut' was actually a doublewide trailer with vinyl siding and a freshly built front deck and steps. Emerick gazed upwards.

"Lookie up there at that *satellite* dish on the roof! Think they're watching Mother Angelica? Thought they were supposed to be praying, meditating and stuff."

The hermitage was at the farthest and highest end of the monastery grounds, just a stone's throw from the county's high heavy-wire fence. Just on the other side of the fence lay state land, Stilton Mountain Forest, the 'heart-break' woods.

"I never realized it," Emerick said, thoughtfully, "But you could sneak off into town from here, if you could figure how to get

47

through that fence." He bent and peered. "And it looks like there's a section down there, peeling away. Hmmmm…"

He then tried to slip the key into the front lock. "Well, darn, I thought this key would open the hermitage up. Maybe someone changed the lock?" To Odo: "Father Lucian used to come up here to pray, and be alone. And probably, work on his book. I was hoping to find some other clue in there."

Odo took from his pocket the sharp little scissors he had taken from the library desk. Once again he inserted the blade in the lock, twisted it this way and that, then swung the door open.

Emerick laughed, in delight. "Hah, hidden talent! You sure come in handy sometimes!"

Erdwulf immediately trotted inside, then quickly began pacing the front room, going into the hall and coming back, as if he were looking for something. Or someone. He began to whine, softly, as if grieving.

"Sorry, poor guy. I know you miss Lucian. You'll see him soon in Heaven, no doubt." Emerick knelt to give him a comforting hug, then stood to look about. The trailer appeared to be spotless inside: rather spacious with a small kitchen, dining area and two comfortable sofas. Edgy, abstract art adorned the walls, which had been painted a cool gray.

"Never been in here before," Emerick remarked. "Not really a place for serious prayer, is it? There's even a big-screen TV! It's more like a ski lodge, or bachelor pad." He walked over to a table, where three chairs were askew, and a pair of squat tumblers sat, a sticky residue of amber in each. Odo stood beside him as he sniffed at the contents.

"Whoa. The good stuff. Jameson's I'd say or real Scotch-scotch." He paused. "Lucian was the serious drinker among us. Not an alcoholic, mind you, not at all, but he appreciated good, expensive, spirit. Guess this is where he came to indulge himself now and then.

Him and I bet…Izzy… Now there's the guy with the drinking problem, my poor ol' boss."

He had just noticed, beside the glasses, a small, overturned pill bottle, an amber pharmacist's cylinder, empty. But the label had been torn off and there were no other clues to the bottle's contents. It made Emerick uneasy to see it, though, remembering Marion's suggestion of a possible overdose on Lucian's part.

"No," he muttered to himself. "Nah, he wouldn't do that, he just wouldn't…" He looked up. "Odo? Erdie? Hey, where'd you guys go?"

He found the younger monk in the bedroom, with Erdwulf at his side. Odo excitedly motioned him over to a bedside table, and showed him an opened drawer. Emerick peered in, and saw a pair of horn-rimmed glasses and an oversized set of Holy Land olive-wood rosary beads. He gazed at them somberly, then at the bed.

"So," he murmured. "How did he get from here, to the forest, without wearing those glasses? He was blind as a bat without 'em."

Odo pulled down the comforter at an angle, stopping short in surprise. A small object lay in the center of the mattress, atop pristine white sheets. Emerick took a deep breath and plucked the small, shining object up. A gleaming, irridescent orb, attached to a golden fish-hook.

"A pearl," he murmured. "An actual pearl, a woman's earring. Because Philbertines don't wear jewelry, that's for sure. And this ain't no Walmart special, neither, I think it's the real deal. I'll have to show it to Momma, she'll know." He closed his fingers around the earring. "This wasn't some local teenage couple sneaking in to borrow the bed. It was a grown-up *guest*."

They heard the front door open. The two monks exchanged a look of surprise.

"Aw, come on, we'll just march on out like we have every right in the world to be here." Emerick strode fearlessly into the living room—Erdwulf at his heels--and suddenly exclaimed—

"Well, well. If it isn't Mister Novice-Master himself!"

Odo ran back into the bedroom and shut the door behind him. He listened through the thin paneled trailer wall:

"And if it isn't the Barefoot Contessa. What the hell are you doing here?"

"I could ask you the same question, Clix. The abbot has officially shut the hermitage down, haven't you heard? And showing up in your civvies, a nice silk shirt there, and a bottle of wine, too? Napa Valley, I bet. Expecting company, Brother? A fine lady who wears pearls, perhaps."

"A *woman?*" He heard Callixtus' low laugh. "Were I to bring anyone here for *illicit* purposes, Brother, it would *not* be a female. Thought you knew that..."

"Just checking."

"I don't believe you have permission to be up here, Emerick."

"Do you?"

There was a moment of silence, before Emerick's good-natured chuckle. "At least *I'm* dressed proper. For prayer and meditation, that is."

"What precisely *are* you doing here?" Callixtus countered. "Is this The Hillbilly Detective, episode one? Has it occurred to you that you've become a tad delusional?"

"Lucian was my mentor, Clix. Yours and mine. He was a good man, and I just don't think he was ready to die. Do you?"

"Look, cowboy, you're not the only one grieving for Lucian. You didn't even work with him. That was me, remember?"

"Yeah, I saw you grieving in chapel yesterday. And yet, you didn't even wait for his body to be washed, before you took over the library."

"How *dare* you? How dare you malign my grieving process! I knew him *better* than you did! I didn't come in to pester him with goose feathers and dirty feet, I *worked* with him, every day! How do you think I feel about it? Do you think I wanted him to die?"

"Certainly hope not."

"Look, you idiot, I will be *not* be one of your suspects!"

"You're not," Emerick's voice expressed surprise. "I don't suspect any of the monks. Thinking its someone from outside, to be honest..."

"Yeah, did you see the hole in the fence?" Callixtus offered. "I complained to both the old and the new abbot. Frederique didn't want to hear anything about it." Just when it seemed his tone toward Emerick was growing more conciliatory, he added: "Grow up, choir boy, and accept the truth. Lucian chose death, for reasons unknown to you or me. You can't change that. Now get out."

"Don't worry, we won't be staying, we were just—Odo!! Where'd you go?!"

Odo scurried from the bedroom, his hands stuffed deep into his habit's chest flap. He shot only the briefest of glances at his 'novice-master' then preceded Emerick out the door.

Emerick frowned, but was silent, as they headed down the steep dirt path back toward the orchard and monastery. Erdwulf hurried ahead, obviously anxious for a nap back at the barn. About mid-way down, as they passed through a copse of black ash, Emerick said: "Well, we picked up at least one more clue, maybe. But, geez, I was not happy to see Callixtus show up like that. I try to be charitable, but man, that guy gets on my last nerve. He has it in for me, for some reason. Probably 'cause of Lucian. Liking me better'n him..." He turned to Odo. "Did you find anything else in the bedroom? Although I suppose we found enough..."

Odo pulled his hand out of his flap and handed a torn sheet of paper to him. Emerick stopped short, as soon as he saw the fan-shaped leaf on it.

"The missing page, from the botanical book?! Where'd you find it?"

Odo mimed pulling up a mattress corner, as if tucking in a sheet.

"Was there anything else there? A cut-off knot, perhaps?"

To Emerick's astonishment, Odo pulled out a wrinkled beige Publix plastic supermarket bag wrapped around a clump of something. Emerick took the bag from him, opened it, and then let out a single, but very foul, curse word.

The bag was filled with *money*: US currency, in large-denominated bills. Emerick looked about, then shoved the bag into his own scapular flap.

"Yikes, Odo! What a thing to find! What are we gonna do with it?"

Odo gave him a faintly mournful look. Emerick stopped and turned back to the mountain. "Maybe we should… put it back? Forget we saw it? No, that would be cowardly…The abbot, we have to tell the abbot.…What in holy *hell* is going on up there? Fornication, big money….*drugs?* Odo, boy, I think we're in over our heads! We have to turn the money over to the abbot and let him decide. I don't know what else we can do."

7.

Dom Frederíque looked wearily at the two young monks sitting on the other side of his desk, both flushed and sweaty, with deeply distressed looks on their faces.

"Dear God, what have you boys done? Something requiring an enormous penance, I'm fearing."

"We done nothing wrong, Dom Frederique. Well, not intentionally. We went up to the hermitage this morning. I knew you wouldn't approve...but I thought there might be some clue about Father Lucian's death up there."

The abbot sighed, deeply. "And did you find such a clue?"

"We found this." He stood up and dumped the plastic bag out: A cascade of green bills fell onto the desk, and the abbot's eyes widened in shock, as he jumped to his feet.

"*Mon Dieu!* So much money!" He looked up at Emerick in alarm. "You found this at the hermitage?"

"Yes, sir. Odo did, under the proverbial mattress. Where some Americans, I should explain, like to keep their savings ..."

"But not monks! Surely a stranger, an invader, left it there! Was there anyone else at the hermitage when you were up there?"

Odo looked expectantly at Emerick, who tilted his head, as if trying to recall. To Odo's surprise, he shook his head slightly.

"Well, what are we to do with this...this *cash*? You have given us a very large problem here, Brothers."

"I'd expect you'd turn it over to the police, sir." Emerick held up his phone. "I've got Ardelle on speed-dial now."

"No!" the abbot barked. "No local authorities. This is private!"

Emerick sat forward. "I understand, Dom Frederique, with all due respect...In your native country, maybe you couldn't trust local law enforcement, but here...They'll know what to do. Ardelle is top-notch, a really sharp lady, and I'm not saying that because she's family. And she's the one who should be investigating this whole thing, along with Lucian's death...Not...not me and Odo here."

"It is the practice of the Philbertines to handle these matters internally." The abbot went to his door. "*Odrian!*" he shouted. "In my office, at once!" Then to the brothers: "I am not sure...he will be able to take this, our sacristan and accountant. He is so very nervous, you know."

Father Odrian, who was indeed the sacristan who prepared the chapel for liturgy as well as the monastery bursar, came rushing in, mouse-like, small, bald and meek, his face dominated by oversized glasses. He stopped short when he saw the money, his lower jaw dropping slightly.

"Brothers Odo and Emerick found this money on monastery property. Brother Emerick is of the mind that we call the local police, but I am sure they will only confiscate it and keep it for themselves. What say you, Father Odrian?"

Odrian gaped at the two younger monks. "Where did you find it?" he whispered.

"Up at the hermitage."

"It is Father Lucian's, perhaps?" the abbot asked. "Did he not use that building also?"

"He did," Odrian murmured. "So did Isidore, Marion, Callixtus, and Father Francis, before his stroke. I don't think it's theirs, Dom. I...I can't begin to imagine what it was doing there..."

"Father, count it. Tell us precisely how much is there."

Reluctantly, Odrian went to the desk and began handling the bills, tentatively, as if each contained a dangerous virus on their surface. He carefully separated the bills into denominations, taking a calculator from his pocket to make the final calculation.

"Thirteen thousand, two hundred forty-seven dollars," he said. The other monks gasped.

"Whoa! You could buy a pretty nice used car with that kind of dough!" Emerick exclaimed.

"What monk has this kind of money!" The abbot asked, incredulously. "It *must* have been left by an intruder!"

"You do know that part of the fence has fallen down, leading to the state forest?" Emerick asked.

The abbot nodded, grimly. "Yes, I recall…Brother Callixtus mentioned something about that…Perhaps I should have looked into it. Is the forest such a very dangerous place, Brother Emerick?"

"Only at night. There's no bears or nothing like that. Maybe a rattler or two. Kids from the high school go up there to scare themselves or make home-made horror movies with their phones. The local drug addicts used to go there to shoot up. Or *did.* I guess they just take pills at home now. And there's the suicides, too, of course, but that's not a real common thing anymore. Still, it would be tempting, I think, to break onto the monastery grounds, 'cause kids from town think the monastery is spooky and weird, too. Can't think why anyone would leave a pile a cash up there, though."

"The crime in this economically depressed area is just *terrible,*" Odrian moaned. "It's got to be an outsider for sure."

"Then don't you agree, Father Odrian," said Emerick, "that we should contact the sheriff's office? I can't seem to convince the abbot."

"Are you nuts?!" Odrian exclaimed. "That could put all of us in *danger*!! Especially if it's drug money! If whoever left it there found out we turned it over to the police…they might kill us all, out of revenge!"

"Then… what do we do with it?"

"Put it back, where you found it!" Odrian screeched.

"No!" the abbot thundered. "We will not be controlled by outside crime. Nor will we go to the local authorities, who I still do not trust completely. For now, we shall place it in the safe here in my office. I alone have the combination, do I not?"

"Yessir," said Odrian, meekly. "It was given to you along with Dom Rasmus's papers. There's a copy of it in a safe deposit box, downtown."

"*You* don't have the combination, being the bursar and all?" Emerick asked him, in a skeptical way.

Odrian shrugged. "We never use it. We have our account at Potomoc Highlands Trust. And we really have nothing of value to put in there. It's just a hole in the wall."

"It is true, I found it completely empty, just after I arrived," said Frederique. "Now move that painting, someone, so we can safely place this enormous money inside."

Odrian went obediently to the portrait of Saint Philbert, who glared back at him in 12th century monastic garb. He swung the painting to one side, and held it up with his shoulder, wincing, as the abbot began twisting the combination lock. Odo, fascinated, sat forward and watched intently as the abbot swung open the door and stuffed the beige plastic bag full of cash inside, then slammed the safe door shut. Odrian gratefully let Philbert swing back into place.

The abbot turned back to Odo and Emerick. "Now. We shall see if someone comes to look for it; and we will act accordingly. Odrian, arrange to have the hermitage hut dismantled and taken off monastery grounds at once. That will send a message, to whoever is using it for illicit purpose. We can only pray no one among our number is involved."

"I have an idea," Emerick spoke up. "Offer it to the Humanity habitat in town. They'll send guys up to take it apart and off the grounds, it'll go to good use. But there was a big old TV and satellite dish—maybe we could keep those and bring them down here?" he asked, hopefully.

"No TV!" the abbot thundered.

"Brother Emerick!" said Odrian, in reprimanding tone. "Do you know how much money the resale of that building could bring in—in the thousands! The monastery could use that money!"

"Are we in the property business now?!" the abbot snapped. "We will donate it to the homeless, as Brother Emerick suggests. And all of its contents. Odrian, see to that matter at once. Now, if that is all—and that is enough, I assure you, for one day—you may return to your chores. What *are* your chores today, brothers?"

"Cidery for me, Odo's going back to peeling his turnip, I guess."

"Devote yourselves to work and prayer the rest of the day, and no more detective work." He suddenly looked up at the door.

"Brother Callixtus. What is it?"

Emerick and Odo turned, warily, to see the 'novice-master' at the door, now dressed in his robes and cowl and only slightly out of breath. He folded his hands together, calmly.

"I thought, perhaps, you might want to see me," he said in a strangely humble manner. He glanced coolly at Emerick and Odo.

The abbot tented his fingers together. "Callixtus, have you been spending any time up at the hermitage lately?"

"I can explain that, sir, I was given the *right* to use it, under the old abbot, I am not violating any rules in going there, I was only—"

The abbot put up his hand. "I am not questioning your use of it, Brother. Not right now. Tell me, did you leave any personal possessions up there, by any chance?"

"Possessions? I'm afraid I don't understand you, abbot."

"Do you keep money up there?"

"*Money?*" he seemed genuinely mystified. "I have no money! Where would I get money?" He turned now to the other brothers. "Did you guys find *money* up there?"

Odo of course remained silent. But so did Emerick, who simply folded his hands together, and looked Callixtus in the eye.

"Who else uses the hermitage, Brother?" the abbot asked.

Callixtus frowned. "Well, Father Lucian used it, but also...I know that Brother Isidore would meet Lucian up there, to talk. Sometimes Brother Marion. And you, too, Father Odrian, I saw you up there once."

Odrian turned scarlet. "I wouldn't leave money there!" he protested. "Not when we have a perfectly good bank in town to store it!"

The abbot sighed. "No one is *accusing* you, Odrian...Nor do I suspect any of our monks. I can only conclude for now, it was left there, by an intruder."

"That's a disturbing thought, isn't it," Callixtus murmured. "Perhaps we should look into some sort of security, Abbot."

"The hermitage is to be dismantled and removed from the grounds, at once." And before Callixtus could register any kind of surprise or protest, the abbot dismissed him. "That is all, Brother. You may return to your work."

Callixtus bowed, but threw a rather fierce sidelong glance at Emerick and Odo before he left.

"Perhaps this matter is settled for now, but I must think long about it. It is time for all of us to return to our work." The three remaining monks rose to leave, but the abbot reached over and caught Emerick by the sleeve.

"Please remain, Brother. I would like to talk to you...alone. Please, close the door."

Emerick did so, then sank back down into the chair opposite the abbot, who looked very serious and somber.

"Brother, I think you need to release yourself from this obsession for truth, and accept Father Lucian's death for what it was...I am not ordering you to, but for your own well-being, I don't think there is anything to be gained by it."

"*What?* You don't see a connection between the money, the hermitage—"

"Perhaps there is, but it's for others to find. May we talk, for a moment, about Brother Odo?"

"What about him?"

"He is an interesting little monk, is he not? It is quite tragic, about the closure of the Quebec abbey. How do you think he is adjusting to our monastery?"

"He seems to fit right in. He seems happy to be here. I have the sense…that's it's a better place than he thought it would be. And probably way better than his situation in Quebec."

"Does he ever *speak* to you?"

"He says a random word now and then. He's able to speak. He just don't. Nothing wrong with his hearing, either."

"Has he told you anything about his former abbey?"

"Well, no. See, he don't actually *talk*."

"I know that! I thought perhaps he communicated to you in some other way…" Frederique rubbed his chin. "What is his *ethnic* background, do you think? Clearly he is not Caucasian."

"Don't matter, does it?"

"Of course not. I am only curious. Do you think he might be an indigenous North American? From one of those *Arctique* tribes?"

"I have no idea. I do see some Asian in him, though."

"He does puts me in mind…of an Ethiopian brother, I once knew…"

"Didn't the monastery in Quebec tell you anything about him?"

"Not very much. That monastery is no more; Odo was their last monk, and the abbot flew off to the French motherhouse, essentially abandoning him. That might be his trauma. He would not remember the trauma surrounding his infancy…"

"What sort of trauma was that?"

"When his abbot, Gervaise, wrote to me—essentially making him my responsibility—"

"Dumping him in your lap."

"Yes, that is a good idiom. He said the boy was brought to the monastery as a very small infant. He said the child was found in a trash bin in the city of Montreal, in the midst of winter. They believe, in fact, the day of his birth was December 25. The infant was thought to be dead at first, then revived at a hospital. There was publicity about it, but no offers for adoption, perhaps because the child was brown, and brain-damage was feared. So he was sent north, to the Philbertine monastery and convent of Notre-Dame-de-Glacier, it was the only home he ever knew. "

"Oh, boy…" Emerick murmured. "Poor kid!"

"Gervaise writes that Odo *never* spoke a word. And he infers that Odo is actually feeble of the mind, brain-damaged in some way. Do you think so, Brother?"

Emerick shook his head emphatically. "Not. At. All. In fact, I think he's *real* smart. He was the one who found the money at the hermitage! I think he understands a lot more than anyone realizes."

"Why do you think it is that he can't—or won't—talk?"

Emerick shrugged. "Don't know, for sure. Maybe no one ever taught him, proper-like. If he had no momma to fuss over him, or sing to him or even yell at him…he'd have to pick it up on his own. That French-Canadian is probably his first language, so maybe his English ain't so good—"

"Nor is yours," said the abbot, archly. "Or, I must admit, mine."

"I'm also guessing—having been in the military and having served overseas—it could be some kind of PTSD thing."

"That is—?"

"Post Traumatic Stress Disorder, sir."

"I see. Do *you* have PTSD, Brother Emerick?"

"What?" He was taken aback. "No, no. *No!* My experiences over there weren't exactly pleasant, but…not hurtful or scarring. To my brain, that is. Did a number on my leg, that's where my injury was. And growing up around here wasn't exactly a picnic, neither. But I'm pretty adaptable—"

"Why did you enter the monastery, Brother?"

"Well, I reckon…I was *called* to it, Dom Frederique."

"In what fashion? The Call comes in different forms, does it not?"

Emerick paused, squirming slightly. "Well, I don't know that I've exactly *heard* it yet, to be truthful. When I first came here, 'bout two years ago now, I know it probably wasn't for the right reasons. Being in operations overseas was pretty stressful, then I was in the VA hospital, and then...I just wanted some peace. I wanted to be with...*good* people. And I practically grew up with this place, with Gramma working in the book shop—well, when you still had the book shop and visitors center here. I told you, I was even baptized in the chapel, as a baby. Well, the old chapel that burnt down. And it was Gramma who brought me here the day I entered, she dropped me off and told Brother Bart to look after me. I know that sounds...lame, but I felt a little weird and bashful, didn't know if the abbey would even take me. But I knew it would be quiet and peaceful-like here. And it is. It's like home now, and truthfully, I don't really think I want to leave this part of West Virginia ever again."

"That is a charming explanation, but it does not sound like much of a vocation, Brother."

"I know. But I haven't left yet, so that means something, don't it? The more I'm here, the more I feel I'm digging in. Still struggling with the spiritual thing, but Lucian...Lucian was helping me with that."

"You have spiritual doubts...?"

"Yeah, well, that's for me to work out. I wouldn't want you to worry about it. You have enough to worry about, just getting used to this place, this country. This part of the country."

"Do you know why I was sent here, Brother?"

"On account of old Dom Rasmus having that heart attack, and dying." And now Emerick's eyes flickered, with some sadness, to the photograph that had just been hung behind the current abbot's desk:

Old, rotund, smiling Rasmus, his blue skullcap skew at a rakish angle atop his head, the long Santa Claus beard tumbling over his prodigious belly, Erdwulf at his side.

"And generally you would elect a new abbot from your ranks. But there were no suitable candidates, were there?"

"Brother Marion stepped in as…a kind of interim abbot, I suppose. Till you came."

"The head of our order sent me here because he was deeply concerned about the *moral* state of your abbey. The American monks, he said, were weak and lazy, too deeply influenced by modern culture; they had fallen away from the spiritual and monastic ideals of Saint Philbert."

"Begging pardon, sir, but, like…how would he know, if he hadn't been here?"

"Obviously, they had received word. I think it's been a concern for years. I think the simple fact that this abbey is in America makes it more susceptible to outside temptations and distractions. Which is why I am having the hermitage taken down, and our Internet account cancelled."

"Well, there's no computers here anyways. And half the time we don't have phone reception so…"

"Never mind that. I was sent here as a reformer. It is not a role I relish, or even desire. Reforming abbots are never respected or admired. But I can see I have my work cut out, as that English idiom goes. This is why I will not call your American police yet, only when I feel I have gained more knowledge of this abbey and its monks. The money you found is going nowhere, it is safe in the wall for now. As for you, Brother Emerick, we will begin the process of your reformation right away, and I believe that will help with your spiritual doubts. First of all, you will begin…by wearing *shoes*!"

"But our founder—"

The abbot put up a warning hand. "That was eight centuries ago! When people carved their shoes from trees! It is foolish and unsafe for you to go about barefoot! You surely do not do so in winter, do you?"

"Well, no, I have sandals or flip flops for the snow."

"You will henceforth be *calced*—I expect to see some kind of footwear on you from now on."

Emerick took on a pained expression. "Please, Dom. I *hate* wearing shoes! I just *can't*...my feet feel all trapped and claustrophobic inside them!"

"Then the wearing of shoes will be your penance, your cross to bear...Give it all up for God, my boy. A healthy monk has much to offer his monastery. And you have much to offer yours. I also think you should consider study, for Holy Orders."

Emerick paled. "The priesthood? *Me*? No way!"

"We *need* more ordained men here, priests. We have enough worker-brothers. I think your military training helps form the basis for possible ordination, and the years of study will help to discipline not only your mind but help erase your uncertainties—"

"I...I just don't feel...*up*, to being ordained."

"Are you saying you're not worthy?"

"Possibly. But not because of anything I've done, or believe. It's...just a really big step. I'm not ready, at all."

"It may turn out that you are completely unfit for the priesthood, but in my mind, this cannot be judged unless you attempt it. I believe you are meant to do more than squeeze apples into alcoholic cider. Ah, that is the other thing. I know you helped Lucian in the library, but henceforth, Brother Callixtus will be in charge there; he says he will not need your help."

"Why don't you make him be a priest? Send him to France for training."

"Speaking of Callixtus, you may also join the Latin class he will be teaching to Brothers Christoph and Odo."

Emerick shut his eyes briefly in silent despair.

"Now you may go," said the abbot, crisply. "Unless there are any other matters."

Emerick stood, and paused. "Father Lucian's eyeglasses and rosary were in the nightstand beside the bed, at the hermitage. Perhaps before it's taken down…someone could retrieve them? The rosary, at least. We don't use it anymore, but he did. It meant something to him."

"The items…you said were missing, when he was found in the forest?"

Emerick nodded, and the abbot considered this for a long moment.

"Very well. I will go and retrieve them myself. But I'll entrust them to you, for safekeeping. Go now, and prepare for Terce. No more detective work today."

8.

When Saturday evening came, and Compline prayers had concluded, beginning the monastic night, Emerick did not return to his room but walked outdoors in the dark toward the cider barn. Odo watched and debated with himself whether or not to follow along; Emerick had not offered his customary inviting wave. But he was curious to see what the other brother would do next.

Emerick was getting into the old pale-green truck, when he caught sight of the younger monk, lingering a few yards away from the garage.

"Just going out for a little bit," he called out, as he started the engine. "To see my big brother Gary over in Spitzville, probably better if you stay—"

But Odo was already making his way into the passenger seat.

"The thing is, I'm not really supposed to leave abbey grounds without telling Abbot or Brother Bart. And neither are you. So get out, please."

Odo would not budge.

"All right then, don't come crying to me when Novice-master gives you latrine duty."

But once they moved toward the main road, he shrugged. "Most of the monks are in bed already and hopefully the abbot, too, and...Well, no harm in a little family visit. Besides I think, for once in his life, my brother might be able to help us out a bit."

He bumped back down the mountain, to the main road where Odo had been left by the Greyhound bus only a week before—and what a week it had been. Emerick steered the truck onto the interstate, zipping along at an alarming speed, with the local country station blaring on the radio, then took the first exit, squealing into the roadside parking lot of the Spitzville-Skerritsville Big Roof Inn, which sat only a few feet from the truck noise and whizzing cars of the interstate. There was only a scattering of cars in the parking lot, and then suddenly there was one more: the red and blue strobing lights of highway patrol.

A burly officer perched himself by Emerick's open window.

"Biff! Not *again*." He roared, his raspy voice filling the interior of the truck. "No warning this time, I'm writing you a ticket!"

Emerick gazed at him, nonchalantly. "Was I *speeding*, Wally?"

"You know you were! At least ten miles over the limit."

"Well, that ain't so bad, is it?"

"How many times is this now?"

"I'm sorry, Wally, as I told you...the speedometer's broke on this thing."

"Then fix it, dammit! I have half a mind to call your abbot—Or, your momma."

"Don't do that, I'm already in deep enough with him. And her. Just this once, let me off…I promise, I'll double up on my prayers tomorrow morning at Mass. I'll pray for you, and your'n."

"That a bribe?"

"Sure, if you want it to be. Best offer you'll get all day! Can't offer you nothing else."

"How about some of that fine old cider of yours. You got a bottle or two in there?"

"It's done sold out. I'll save you a few bottles from the next batch, I promise."

"Deal." He suddenly turned serious. "That was something, wasn't it, that monk of your'n, up yonder on the mountain this week."

"You were there, huh?"

"Well, sure. You think he really done himself in, like Ardelle says?"

"I do *not!* I told her, he was *murdered!*"

"You know, when I saw him, I kind of thought the same thing. I was lookin' at those marks and bruises around his neck… didn't seem like a natural suicide hanging, you know."

"Right?! Everyone thinks *I'm* crazy!"

"And also, his face. Usually when folks die like that, you don't want to look at their faces afterwards. But he seemed kinda…composed, like. Like someone fixed him up a little, afterwards."

"Yes, *yes!* I was trying to explain that to Brother Marion!"

"Think maybe it was another monk who done it?"

"Can't believe that, Wally. Violent men as a rule don't enter monasteries. And we *are* a group of good, steady guys. I'm pretty sure it was somebody on the outside. Random, maybe. But sick. You of all people know how much crime there is around here."

"Not as much as you think anymore. See, with the crack cocaine and the meth, there was a lot more, because it got people buzzed up to go out and be violent. But these opioids—well, they just knock people out or put them to sleep."

"Still…addiction forces people to do terrible things."

"Can't argue with that." He stepped back from the truck. "Look…get that damn speedometer fixed already." He hit the side of the truck and began to turn away. "Oh, and tell Gary I said 'hey.'"

Odo marveled at the instant coolness—indeed, sheer coldness—that hit them both as they strode through the automatic doors and into the motel. The abbey, of course, had no air conditioning, only a few battered fans, and there had been no need for either at Notre-Dame-de-Glacier, which was always very cool, even indoors in winter.

Gary Ottlesby, the Big Roof's night manager, lay partly slumped over the front desk, idly poking at his cellphone. He resembled Emerick slightly, with the same hue of sandy hair and blue eyes, but his face was longer, thinner, sharper. He wore a bright red shirt with a strangely luminescent green-blue tie, and his hair stood up in stiff, shiny spikes; one of his eyebrows was pierced with a tiny gold ring. Emerick stood on the other side of the counter for a long minute, surreptitiously moved the silver domed call bell close to his brother's ear and dinged it emphatically. Gary jumped.

"Christ, Biff, you scared the bejeezus out of me!"

"Don't use our Lord's name in vain, you jerk. Don't you have anything to *do* around here?"

"Water main break. Can't give out any rooms. I'm just keeping an eye on the bar, but man, it's slow for a Saturday. Hey, you can't come in here barefoot you know."

In response, Emerick lifted the hem of his robe, and showed off his flip-flops: Powder blue, with a huge plastic rose in the center of each foot. Gary snickered.

"Where'd you get them? Dollar General?"

"They're Gramma's! She left them at the abbey last time she come visit."

"You're not like...naked under that thing, are you?"

In response, Emerick lifted his robe a little higher, showing off knee-length madras-plaid swim trunks. At the same time, Odo saw his left leg, deformed by harsh scar tissue and healed-over burns. "Guess the pool's out of the question, huh?" Emerick asked, plaintively.

"Yeah. Anything with water. Don't you have Whispers or Sextants or whatever those prayers you have to say all day long?"

"Done for the day." Emerick let his skirts drop. "Did you record episode seven of *Red Viking Crusader* for me?" he asked, in reference to a cable-channel miniseries set in the same medieval era as his order's founding.

"Um...was that the one where Ragnok ties Lord Nerander to an iron pole and roasts him over the bonfire, then eats his liver?"

"Damn! Thanks for the spoiler, bro."

"Don't tell me they did crap like that, in the old Saint Philbert days."

"Oh sure, why ol' Philbert himself...You know they sliced him open, tied one end of his intestines to a team of horses—"

"Yikes! Who did that, the Saracens?"

"No, unfortunately it was monks from a rival monastic order—"

"How can you be part of this sick, medieval crap?!

"I'm *not*. I'm part of this sick, modern, contemporary crap, like everyone else. Frankly, not liking it very much right now."

"Finally had it with the monastery, huh?"

"No. It's the world outside the monastery...that's creeping in."

Gary looked over at his companion. "That...the new guy?"

"This is Odo, from Quebec. He don't talk much."

"Frodo? Like Lord of the Rings or whatever?"

"*Odo*, you dunce." Emerick put his hands on the counter. "Odo was Saint Philbert's most trusted companion. It's the second-best Philbertine name you can have. Odo, this is my older brother, Gary. But just barely; he's only nine months older than me."

"Irish twins," Gary muttered. " 'Cept we ain't Irish."

"And Maggy is my true twin, just two minutes older than me. Boy Momma was sure busy back then, wasn't she?" He chuckled, ruefully.

"We were all baptized at the old Holy Face chapel, but it didn't take for Gary." Emerick glanced toward the TV in the lounge, tuned into an evangelical channel. A red-faced, heavyset man was imploring his audience to turn to the Lord NOW.

"You watching this?"

"Hell, no." Gary grabbed for the remote. "Bad enough having *you* here. Go on and sit down, I'll grab us some Cokes."

"And some chips, too. Got any of those triple-fudge-chocolate ice cream bars?" Emerick leaned over the counter, hopefully, on tip-toes.

"Don't they feed you at that monastery?"

"We don't get *treats*."

"Out of ice cream, just chips and pop," said Gary, coming from around the desk and flopping onto a sofa in the lounge. He clicked the remote to the Weather Channel. "Look, we're having one of them dangerous heat waves again. Great time for the pool to be broke."

Odo looked at his icy bottle of Coke as if it were an alien object, then with some surprise at the TV, where the entire US temperature map was glowing in fiery shades of orange and yellow.

"Didn't you record any of *Red Viking* for me?" Emerick asked, plaintively. "How 'bout episode eight?"

"That was a pretty lame episode," Gary continued. "Where they sail to this island and there's lots of romance and nudity and stuff you probably shouldn't be watching."

69

"I can watch it, I just can't *do* it. That reminds me, I wanted to ask you something. Has to do—in a way—with, um…all that."

"You mean *sex*? You want me to finally explain it to you, little brother?" Gary chortled. "Here's how it goes. A man and a woman meet, and they decide they love each other very, very much—"

"Shut *up*!" Emerick shoved him. "You don't know any more about it than I do!"

"Hah! Bet I do! *I'm* not a monk!"

"Well…You ever heard any rumors about…randy stuff, going on at the monastery?"

Gary's eyebrows shot up. "There is?!"

"Not that I know of…But I don't always know what people outside the abbey say about the abbey. I just assume they think we're mighty strange men, and you know people around here like to gossip and tell tales. I was just wondering if you heard any. Maybe a story about our hermitage?"

"Your *what*? Isn't that in Russia?"

"*Our* hermitage, not The Hermitage. It's a little hut we have in the woods—"

"Where you could sneak off and have, like, orgies, stuff like that? Watch porn? *Make* porn? No, I never heard any stories like that about your monastery. Sounds like fun, though, if true."

"No! Don't *want* it to be!"

"Why would you ask me about it then? You think something's going on up there, behind your back? Hey, don't you feed that guy back at the abbey?"

Odo had already polished off the chips, and was making his way through a bowl of complimentary M&Ms; it looked like he would finish them soon.

"Leave him be. Don't think they fed him much, up in Quebec," said Emerick. "Look, did you hear about our Father Lucian?"

"Who?"

"Don't you ever read the newspaper?"

"What paper? We only have *USA Today*, now. They don't report much on our neck of the woods."

"Local news on TV??"

"Was it on there?"

"How would I know? You're the one out in the world, not me. But you seem pretty clueless about it."

"What happened to Father Lucian?"

"He died. He died in a very strange way. They found him…well, Odo here and I found him…on Stilton Mountain. In the Heart-break Forest. With his own cord around his neck."

"Whoa!" Gary nearly dropped his Coke. "A priest committing suicide! He's going to hell for sure, right?"

"That's the thing, I don't think he did it. I think he was *murdered.*"

"Double whoa! That's even crazier! Who would murder a monk! Another monk?"

"No! Not the way that's supposed to work. But that's what I'm trying to figure out. I have only the weirdest clues: One of the knots from his cord got cut off, that's where I think the sex comes in. Because the knot represents…"

"*Sex?!*"

"No! Chastity! Sexual purity, a completely foreign concept to you, I would guess."

"Thankfully, yes."

"Then we found…well, we found some stuff at the hermitage, the place I mentioned. A woman's earring, in the bed. And not on the pillowcase, but, you know, lower down…"

"Oooh," Gary murmured, appreciatively.

"Then we found this." He pulled the botanical-book page out of his pocket, unfolded it and showed it to his brother. "You have any idea what this plant is?"

Gary regarded it thoughtfully. "Yeah, I know what that is. Remember when I dated that crazy gal from Pigeon Forge, Tennessee? She got me into herbs. Natural medicine. That there is…something called ginseng." He pronounced it *gin-sssang*.

"One of those natural-type herbs?"

"Oh yeah, it's a big-time thing. Or it was. Not so much anymore. It's for…well, funny telling a monk this. Even funnier telling my kid brother. It's a *man*-herb."

"A man-herb?"

"You know. For your you-know-what. So you can do you know-what?"

Emerick balled his fists. "Don't use *euphemisms* with me! I'm a monk, not a eunuch!"

"Easy, boy. You eunuchs are supposed to be non-violent. Anyway, it's an herb supposedly for men."

"What's it do? Help with performance? Or what, impotence?"

"Some say so, but…well, how would I know? *I* wouldn't have any reason to try it. For *that*."

"Would it cure prostate problems? Cancer?"

"Don't know. If it did…wouldn't they use it? The doctors, I mean."

"Maybe. The old infirmarian, they say, used herbs and natural remedies, then sent folks to the hospital when he couldn't figure it out. Brother Marion wants nothing to do with natural medicine; he's got a pill for everything. So this does sort of make sense. But not the sense I want it to make. I don't know how to connect it with Father Lucian. But I'm starting to think he might not be the pure soul I thought he was." He showed the picture again to Gary. "This stuff grow 'round here?"

"Don't think so, think it's Chinese, or something. When you get it in the store, it usually has Chinese letters or writing on it."

"Hah! So you *have* tried it!"

"Hey, it has other purposes! Not just *that*!"

"Perhaps he was trying to obtain it somehow..." Emerick murmured. "Or was researching it. Maybe he thought it was a cure. But how does it lead to him being *dead*?"

"Are you, like, the monastery detective now?"

"No, I'm..." He drew himself up. "I'm more of a *sleuth*. I read enough of them mysteries and detective stories when I was laid up in the VA hospital. There's a difference. A sleuth solves real mysteries, and don't spy on women coming out of cheap motels, like Dad did. But mostly I want to clear Father Lucian's name. I'm afraid though, I'm only going to end up dragging it through the mud."

"You think maybe there's some kind of crime involved?"

"Yeah, I'm pretty sure. Can't go into details, but...oh yeah. Big time."

"Well, you know who to talk to about that."

Emerick glanced over at Odo, who had fallen into a stuporous nap against one of the sofa cushions, the empty M&M bowl still on his lap. He brushed potato-chip crumbs off Odo's cowl in a brisk, paternal way, and turned back to Gary. "I am *not* going to go see Dad," he said in a low voice.

"Just saying..."

"He's all the way across the state! And besides, I don't want to be asking Abbot for permission to make the trip, I don't want him to know I got a father serving a twenty-year prison sentence for fraud and theft. I'm not sure he thinks very highly of me as it is."

"Well, someone should talk to him sometime. We haven't seen him since grade school. Don't he get out soon?"

"Leave him out of this, okay?" said Emerick, wearily. "I have enough things to worry about."

"Still thinking of leaving the monastery?"

"I gotta be honest, with Lucian gone...Maybe. But I can't think about that now, I need to find out what really happened to him. Then

73

maybe I can decide. I'm not...*un*happy there. I like being there. I'm beginning to feel I *should* be there but...Still don't know what I'm really meant to *do* there. Sure wish the Big Guy would give me a sign. Abbot thinks I should be a priest."

Gary laughed out loud, briefly awakening Odo.

"That's *hilarious*! It's a joke, right?"

"What's so funny about it?"

"Me, calling you 'Father.' Which, by the way, I will never, ever, do."

"Not asking you to. Hey, by the way, before I leave...you ever know anyone from the Mecklinburg family?"

"The one whose house burnt up and it turned out the oldest son killed the parents and then set the fire, but he died and only the younger brother survived. I guess you were overseas when that happened..."

"That was the Mecklinburgs?! I knew that name sounded familiar!"

"I knew the older brother, he was a psycho. They put the younger kid in foster care, I think...Jamie, his name was."

"He'd be about eighteen, nineteen now? Big kid? Red hair?"

"Yeah."

"He's our new novice! We call him 'Christoph' now."

"No way! What's he like?"

"Seems normal. Quiet-like. A little goofy. But he works hard in the infirmary, seems to like it. Not sure why he wants to be a monk, though."

"Obviously the trauma, dim-bulb. Isn't that why you went in?"

"I don't have PTSD! Why does everyone think I do?"

"You were in a pretty rough part of the world. You got wounded pretty bad."

"Wasn't hurt all that bad, I was just...knocked out-a commission for a while."

"Almost lost your leg!"

"Other guys ended up a lot worse."

"Yeah, but when you first come back…" Gary frowned. "You were *weird*. All turned inside yourself, so quiet and all …Gotta say, you seem almost normal now, like your old goofy self. So maybe that monastery is good for you."

"Yeah well, old Biff was kind of a screw-up, wasn't he? This guy, Emerick, a little less of one." Emerick rubbed his brow. "But losing Lucian, that was a big blow, a big thing to deal with. He was like…my center, my wing guy to help me through it all. Don't know that I wanna stay there, without him…"

"Then you gotta find out, who done him in."

Emerick looked at his older brother. "I do, don't I? Then I can figure out, what's what."

"Well go do it!"

Emerick jumped up. "Yeah, I better get this kid home. Matins and Lauds is only a few hours away, we gotta go." He started gently pulling Odo to his feet. "I'll give Momma your love," he added. "She's coming up to the abbey tomorrow with Gramma. It's her birthday, she'll be really ticked off that we're not taking her out to dinner."

"Maggy goin' to be there?"

"She's doing the cooking. Her famous fried chicken. And peach pie."

"Be worth it to go for that. But I can't deal with Momma right now. Hey, let me know how you make out, boy detective."

Emerick pushed his young companion toward the double-door entrance. The tall panes of glass parted silently, and they merged instantly from the artificial Arctic into the muggy, wet-blanket heat of a mid-Appalachian night.

9.

Late-night Matins was Odo's favorite liturgy: It came at 3:30 in the morning, with the mournful *dong-dong-dong* bell cutting through the darkness, and there seemed something both exciting and illicit about rushing to chapel at that hour. Once the monks had settled themselves in their seats, all the lights were turned out but for a single candle, illuminating the face of Native-American Mary and her little brown baby. The monks sang to her in the dark, a sleepy, tender, if slightly off-key, song asking for her mercy and help.

Odo did not sing, but listened each night carefully to the words, committing them to heart. He loved the brown Mary, as opposed to the pale blonde Virgin of Quebec; this American woman seemed like she could be his actual mother and he loved, too, the other monks' love and reverence for this woman of color and her little son. He believed that Mary the Virgin was pleased with the monks' humble serenade to her, and would indeed help and comfort them as they asked. Perhaps she would help Brother Emerick in his quest as well.

At daybreak, on the mown front field of Holy Face monastery, Brother Bart set up the lawn chairs for Sunday visitors. Very few came to Holy Face Abbey these days. Brothers Odrian, and Damascene, from Pennsylvania and Maryland respectively, occasionally had family come up. Brother Bart had outlived any local visitors he might have. But no one else had visitors as frequently as Brother Emerick.

That afternoon, he sat beside his mother—they let Gramma have the recliner-chair—while Odo sat on a spread-out patchwork quilt with Emerick's twin sister Maggy—Sister Magdalena Veronica from Holy Face's tiny sister convent, the cloistered nuns of Saint Ethelda, a little further down the mountain. Maggy's convent was in even more reduced circumstances than Holy Face, down to a mere four Sisters, three elderly and mostly infirm, and Maggy, who did all the work but somehow didn't seem to mind. She explained it thus: "We're just a little ol' family; I'm the momma and the three other Sisters are like my daughters, who need lots of caring-for." But she was happy for the occasional escape, this time to celebrate her own mother's birthday. She spread out a down-home feast she had prepared in the convent kitchen: Fried chicken—a treat for the Philbertines who followed a vegetarian diet in accordance with their founder—potato and macaroni salads, home-made pickles and peach pie for dessert. Odo gazed at the feast with saucer eyes.

"Go ahead, fella, dig in!" Maggy encouraged him brightly. She was soft, round, plump, and shorter than her twin, clad in the palest of soft cream-beige, old-style veil and long robe—she reminded Odo of the sweet dumplings they had, sometimes, at Christmas up at Notre-Dame-de-Glacier. The veil covered most of her honey-brown hair, but her bright-blue eyes, much like Emerick's, flashed at him in a way that both delighted and frightened him. "Bet you didn't get this kind of spread up at Old Lady of the Ice up north there! Biffy, you eat, too. I brought the hot sauce for you."

"In a minute." He leaned toward his mother. "Let me show you something. You worked at that jewelry store in the mall." He held out his palm: In the middle was the pearl earring he and Odo had found, at the hermitage.

Doris Ottlesby peered down at it, her lips tightly pursed. She had been, as a young woman, quite lovely, blond and petite, but had grown hard around the edges as she aged. Her blue eyes had turned gray, and dark shadows and wrinkles had pooled beneath them, the accumulation of years of hard work and heartbreak, and two divorces. But she still took care with her appearance, her golden-tinted hair twisted up in back and slightly teased at the crown, her earlobes sparkling with pendulous zircons.

"Where's the other one?" she snapped.

"Only found the one."

"Is that my birthday present?" She looked faintly appalled.

"No, it's part of this…research…I'm doing. But maybe I'll let you have it afterwards. Just tell me if that's a genuine pearl, or not."

In response, Doris picked up the shimmering orb, put it to her lips and let her teeth slide on it a little. "It's the real thing all right. One of them South Seas Pearls, we called them. These earrings set someone back a few bills. Twenty-four karat gold, too. How'd you come by it, son?"

"Believe it or not, we found it on monastery grounds, Odo and me. In a place women ain't supposed to be."

Maggy looked both delighted and scandalized. "In somebody's room, was it?"

"At the hermitage!"

"Oh Lordy, don't tell me that nonsense is starting up again." Maggy slapped the side of her face.

"Well, that's what I aim to find out. I'm sure it has something to do with Father Lucian's passing."

"That monk who died last week?" Doris raised her eyebrows. "Read something about it in the weekly shopper."

"What did they say about him?" Emerick asked, urgently.

"Found him in the woods? I don't know, heart attack? Stroke? Don't let's be talking about that now," Doris said, irritably. "I got enough to be worrying about. Enough bad news in the world—Hey! Are things that bad, in this here monastery, that monks are going around dropping dead?"

"They say it was *suicide*, Momma," Maggy murmured, softly and mournfully.

"Well ain't that awful," Doris murmured, in a low whisper. "A holy man, doing himself in."

"The truth is," Emerick interjected. "*I* think Father was killed and then made to look like he done himself in."

"How come they didn't put that in the paper then? They made it sound like natural causes."

"I think cousin Ardelle soft-pedalled it a bit. I think she's saying 'unknown cause' for now."

"Well that side of the family…they was always the fibbers." She turned wearily to her own mother, who seemed oblivious to the conversation—perhaps because her hearing aid had fallen out. "Momma!" Doris yelled. "Put your hearing thingie back in. Don't you got something for Biff?"

Now Beula sat up from the recliner, fiddling with her ear. "Well, I know it's your birthday, daughter, but I got something for you, boy." She handed over a lumpy package, wrapped in Star Wars wrapping paper. Emerick pulled out thick, fuzzy woolen scarf, full of dropped stitches but done up in Philbertine blue.

"He's your favorite for sure, ain't he!" Maggie laughed, in a merry way.

"I'm working on yours now, granddaughter. Pink and turquoise like you asked for."

Emerick wrapped the scarf around his neck, grinning, then immediately took it off. "Thank, Gramma. This will come in real handy next January, I'm sure."

"Well, ever since I moved in with your momma, all I can do is just knit, knit, knit. Nothin' else to do—"

"Don't start, Ma," Doris muttered. "You hated that assisted living place, so you got no where else to go now."

"Maybe I'll move in with my grandson and live here at this old monastery!" Beula Davies was in her mid-seventies, but still spry, plain-spoken and alert. A tiny, freckled woman, dressed smartly in matching aqua tunic and pants, the tunic trimmed with white daisies. Her snow-white hair was pulled back into a braid that hung to the small of her back, and rimless bifocals sat perpetually on the very tip of her nose. She was a fierce and devoted Catholic, very much a minority faith in Skerritville—as were the Jews and Muslims. She resisted the siren call of the enormous and shiny new Evangelical Church of Christ just built on the outskirts of town, and faithfully attended daily Mass at tiny St. Monica's in Port Gelding, hobbling up the lane with her blue-painted walker. "I know, I know…no women! But I wouldn't bother nobody, not at my age!"

"I'm quite sure," Emerick said, slyly, "Brother Bart would be mighty pleased to let you share his room with him."

"That old coot! He was a nuisance in grade school, and he's still a nuisance, all this time later."

"Aww, Gramma, he's just sweet on you. He's gonna stop by and say hi."

"I hope he don't."

"Grammy!" Maggy's voice was faintly reprimanding. "How come you don't like him? He such a sweet old guy!"

"Sweet! Let me tell you about that boy. I went out with him once, on a hayride, when we was in high school. I knew he was fixing to join the monks, so I figured I was safe. Didn't he try to kiss me and put his hand under my shirt? I slapped him so hard he fell right off that hay-truck!"

Emerick and Maggy doubled over with laughter. Even Doris smiled a bit.

"Don't tell me he'd be any different now!" Gramma concluded.

"Oh, I think sixty years or so in the monastery might've made a difference," said Emerick, with a grin. "Now Gramma, he's looked after me good these past few years, like you asked him to."

"I know, and I'm beholden to him for that. But not enough to let him take advantage."

"You could come and live with us, Grams," Maggy suggested, gently.

"Oh, no offense, darlin', but I couldn't live with a bunch of nuns!"

Emerick leaned over and reached for a plate. "Might be safer with them, Gramma. Hey, we better eat some of this before the ants arrive."

Beula gazed fondly back at the abbey building where she used to work, years ago. "I suppose you're all still mostly goodly men, ain't you now?"

"I'd like to think so," Emerick replied, wistfully.

After the picnic, they all sat back, contentedly, enjoying the sultry beauty of a late Sunday summer afternoon in the mountains. Emerick was simply relieved that neither his mother nor grandmother had remarked on Odo's lack of speech…or his color. They all sat silent for some time, but it was a sweet, lazy and natural sort of silence. Emerick and Odo had been excused from the day's liturgy after morning Mass, and Emerick knew that the other monks were casting envious glances out the window at the front lawn, at him with his family and good food; and he didn't feel one bit bad about that.

"That was good pie, Maggy," said Gramma. "But you ought've peeled the peaches first."

"More fiber," said Maggy, firmly. "We all need it."

"That reminds me." Emerick pulled the ginseng-leaf page from his pocket; the page was becoming quite raggedly and worn now. "Gramma, you ever see this plant anywhere around here?"

Beula tilted up her glasses. "Why, that's 'sang. Oh my, haven't seen that in ages. Oh, sure, we used to dig it up in the hills, and sell it at the Mennonite market. My parents practically made a living at it. See, this particular plant, see how its leaves are crinkly there at the edge. It's a special kind of sang, only grows in this part of West

Virginia, in this part of the mountains. It's supposed to be extra strong, good quality!"

"But what's it *for*?"

Odo, meanwhile, listened from a few feet away, as Maggy began to measure him for his new cotton-linen-blend habit, which she offered to make for him. He stood with his arms stretched out, crucifixion style, and somehow, she managed to measure him without touching him, once. But he still felt a little shiver of delight, at the very nearness of her.

"What's it *for*?" Beula crowed. "What's it *not* for? It's good for everything! It's a regular spring tonic, just makes you feel more invigorated, more pep, everything. Come to think on it, I should start brewing up some sang tea for myself—"

"Oh, no!" Doris interrupted sternly. "With all the meds you take—remember when you ended up in the hospital, after that crazy root tonic you made for yourself."

"Why 'sang is pretty much harmless, darlin', no harm to it. It did work wonders for some folk though. Trouble is, we dug it all up, ain't no more left in the forests no more. I think they had to bring in that Oriental stuff. Or that weaker stuff, from Tennessee."

"Can't you plant it or farm it?"

"Ah, no, you gotta go out and collect it wild in the deep of the woods. It can't be tamed, it's a wild plant; it don't like people. It hides, in the deepest darkest spots. And it's the roots, you know, that are the most valuable; it takes years and years for them to get to proper size. But this is what happens when you just take and take and take from the good earth, and don't give nothin' back."

"Yep, true that," said Emerick. "Well, thanks, Gramma. You've been mighty helpful. Didn't realize this was a local species, although I expected maybe it was."

"What does this all have to do with anything?" Doris asked, irritably.

"Don't know yet," Emerick replied. "But I hope to, soon."

"Look, we have to go," said Doris now, rising from her chair. "I'm sure you boys got your prayers, and it's going be Gramma's bedtime soon. Thanks for a lovely birthday," she said, although Emerick seemed not at all sure she meant it.

"Sorry, Momma," he said, "Gary and Maggy and I will take you out for dinner one night real soon. But Gary's gotta pay for it."

"The least you and your sister could do," Doris snapped. "Thirty-six excruciating hours I spent pushing you two into the world, nearly dyin', all so you could both end up sealed away from the world on this mountain! I don't mind Maggy taking the veil, but I swear, you two boys...I don't know which is worse, you or Gary. I thought I was going to have a couple of good family men, grandchildren by now, to support me in my old age."

"*Momma!*" Maggy admonished her. Emerick simply shrugged, in a wounded way. "Sorry we're such a disappointment to you."

"Oh, it's your daddy's doing, I know that. How was I to finish raising you all proper when he was in prison so long." She frowned at him. "At least Gary...he still has a chance to turn it around. But you...I tell you, a well-adjusted man don't go into a monastery. In this day and age."

A flash of anger crossed Emerick's face. "Don't you be laying any kind of guilt trip on me! It was you making me go into the Army. 'Go in the army and grow up,' you says, it'll make a man out-a you. So I went into the army, got shipped across the world and got blown up for my trouble! I'm not taking any more suggestions from you, lady. I'm living my life the way I need to now, doing what I gotta do!"

"Leave him be, Doris," said Beula. "You gave two children back to the Lord. You should be proud."

"I know, I know..." Doris suddenly leaned over and pressed her face against her son's. "Oh, I love you, baby boy, you know that, you know that, right? I just worry...I just worry, all the time."

Odo, who had been thinking Emerick and his mother did not like each other very much, was startled by the sudden moment of intimacy and affection between mother and son; it gave him an odd, queasy, feeling in the pit of his stomach. Not jealousy, actually, but a kind of yearning.

"I know, Momma." Emerick gave her a little smile, then put his hands on her shoulders. "I'm *fine* here. Don't worry. If anything, it's probably the best place I can be, for now."

"That woman drives me completely round the bend," Emerick remarked later to Maggy, once Doris and Beula had left. The three of them, two Brothers and one Sister, now sat crosslegged on the patchwork quilt together, picking at the remains of the outdoor meal, as late afternoon began to wane into dusk; the fading light seem to add a hearth-like coziness. Emerick suddenly turned to Odo.

"You're right, it *is* better than not having a mother at all."

Odo nodded, knowingly.

Maggy raised an eyebrow so high, it nearly disappeared under her veil. "You *know* what's he's thinking?"

Emerick shrugged. "Sometimes... Never thought about it."

Maggy looked at the younger monk. "Is this true, Odo? Does Biff here seem to know exactly what you're thinking sometimes, even though you can't say it?"

Odo nodded, yes, as if this were perfectly natural.

"Can you tell what he's thinking?"

Odo screwed up his face a bit, as if trying to figure this out.

"We don't catch everything from each other," Emerick replied. "And I guess I'm a lot more unpredictable." He turned to Odo. "Trust me, you wouldn't always want to know what's in my brain sometimes!"

"It's like you got that twin thing, 'cept with him instead of me!"

"I guess..." Emerick looked confused.

84

"Biff! You two got a special gift, you realize? You can read *souls*!"

"What? What are you talking about?"

"It's a *thing*, trust me. Many of the saints could do it. It's been written about." She paused, now a bit uneasily. "Can you read other people, too? Uh...not *me*, though, right?"

"What? No...no. I don't ever know what you're thinking. Never know what's coming out of your mouth next. Or Momma, or Gary... and especially, our new abbot."

"Don't make light of it. It's a genuine gift, from God. Odo must have been sent here, as part of that plan. Because you were meant to connect, somehow, with him. For some reason."

"Oh, brother. Mags, that's old-Church stuff, it's practically superstition!"

"Really?" She drew herself up. "You think I'm Old-Church? Just 'cause I still wear my habit? I can't be bothered with modern clothes, 'specially the way they are now."

"I know, I understand. I understand *you*. We still do have that twin thing going, Maggy, sometimes."

"I know you been troubled by Father Lucian's death. I wish you wasn't."

"Why do you say that?"

"Don't think he's all so...*deserving* of it."

"Maggy, he was my spiritual mentor, you know that. He was such a good man---what? Why are you making that face? You didn't even know him!"

"I can't explain it. I know you say he's a good man and all—but I'm not *feeling* it."

"Why? Do you know something bad about him? Hear something about him?"

"No. But after I heard the news, when I tried to think about him, pray for him...I felt *nothing*. I just don't know...if he's worthy, of your efforts."

"You think he committed suicide?"

"I'm not saying that, although…Despair is a powerful bad thing."

"But he wasn't in despair, he wasn't, I know that—"

"Did he tell you that?"

"No. He wouldn't. I just know."

"How? Did you have the same gift with him, that you have with Brother Odo?"

Emerick was struck silent for a while. "No, it was different. Lucian could speak for himself. But he didn't talk about inner feelings or emotions. I could just…*sense* them. And just before he died, I had a strong sense that he was trying to work out some kind of problem, and he felt he was close to the solution. It was just within his grasp." Emerick held out his own hand, then balled it into a fist. "But the solution wasn't hanging his cord around his neck, I know that."

"I believe you, brother, because I respect your gift," Maggy replied quietly. She then gazed at Odo. "And I believe you, too, have gifts, Brother Odo. I do believe one day…the gift of speech will be bestowed on you. And I betcha anything you won't be able to stop talkin'!"

Odo felt himself blush so deeply, the underside of his skin seemed to burn. But he also felt a secret delight, at Maggy's words.

When Maggy left and the sun had gone down, a pleasing coolness settled onto the mountain. The two young Brothers lay on their backs, side by side, gazing up at the ultramarine sky above, dotted with the stars that could not be seen in the city.

"I wish you could talk," said Emerick wistfully. "I don't want to be talking *at* you all the time. I want to hear, what you would have to say. At least you could tell me to shut up now and then. I wish I knew more about you and your abbey in Canada, your childhood, growing up in that place. Was it an orphanage, actually?"

"No." A tiny word Odo sent, in a tentative way, out into the night air.

"Were you the only kid there, with all them brothers and nuns?"

Odo scrunched up his face, then shrugged.

"I got it, there was a school or something there...But you were the only young-un living at the abbey."

"Yes." And Odo turned to Emerick, who could see he wanted to say more, almost desperately, but couldn't, yet.

"I don't want to pry, but...it wasn't one of those bad places, was it, you weren't like...*abused*, in any way, were you?"

"No..." said Odo, again, but it sounded so tentative and uncertain, it gave Emerick pause.

"I'm committed to our faith, but some of the goings-on, in some corners of it, are pretty awful..." Emerick continued. "But there's still a lot good left in it, which I'm hoping to find here. Because I'm pretty sure this is where I belong. Father Lucian said I just needed to be still, and then I would know...things. Just laying here like this, looking up at heaven, I feel like that's possible. But I still feel so prickly and restless inside, not a good way for a monk in a monastery to be. I can't seem to get *contemplative*—"

"Hey!" Brother Bart's voice cut across the yard, through the darkness. "You boys git them chairs and stuff back in here! No more lollygagging!"

"So much for contemplation." Emerick sighed and sat upright, as did Odo. "Gonna have to find my silence and thinking time somehow..."

10.

The next morning, just after breakfast, Odo was sent to study Latin with Brother Callixtus, but Emerick did not join them. He walked out, alone, to the orchards. Early morning, he felt, was the best time of the day, fresh and cool and quiet; he wanted to check the progress of the early apples—now full-sized but still acid green, tightly crowded on old, gnarled branches. He flicked off a few fat Japanese beetles, who relentlessly munched tiny holes in the leaves. Mostly, he just wanted to think: About the whole puzzle of Father Lucian, the missing knot, Gramma's story about local "sang". The pearl earring, the page torn from the botanical, the money in the hermitage. How did it all fit together? He gazed beyond the orchard, at the wooded slope leading to the hermitage: He'd suspected at first some crime-ring connection with the ginseng, but Gramma said it was all gone. And it couldn't be farmed or replanted...

He found himself walking toward the buzzing of the monastery hives. Brother Asaph, the beekeeper, sat on a bench nearby, about to don his bee-helmet and hood. He was considerably older than Emerick, completely bald, but with a long, luxuriant beard of gold-tinged brown that was the envy of all the monks. He wore a shortened version of the Philbertine habit, with white painter's paints underneath.

"Those apples are coming in just fine, Brother," he called out to Emerick cheerfully, his words laced with cadences of southern Indiana, his home. "Looks like we'll have a bumper crop for autumn cider. Wasn't sure with the hot spell we had, and the lack of rain."

Emerick sank down, in a heavy way, next to Asaph, who put his helmet aside.

"What's up with you? Still torn up about Lucian?"

Emerick turned to him. "Of course I am! He hasn't been underground more'n a week! And buried in that potters field, not with the rest of the brothers. I'm *sure* he was killed. I don't why or how, but I'd sure like to know one way or another."

"What difference does it make? He ain't no Lazarus. He's not coming back, boy."

Emerick flushed slightly. "Don't talk like that, Asaph. Seems...disrespectful."

"Look, we're religious men, aren't we? Death is no punishment or horror, but the gateway to Paradise, you know that. New life. Lucian has found his peace."

Emerick gave him a doleful look. "I know all that," he said, sullenly. "Just don't seem right, is all. His dying, like that."

"You know I'm a practical man." Asaph set a hand on his hip, as he usually did when holding forth. "We all live together here, in community. We all know each other, how can we not? And yet, we *don't*, sometimes. There's always secrets."

"He didn't seem like that kind of man..."

"Look, I could tell you something dark about Lucian. I hate to tell you, 'cause I know you felt very highly about him. I know, for instance, that he was carrying *on*. With a woman, from town."

Emerick shifted himself on the bench. "Not as surprised by that as you might think. But how do *you* know about it?"

"Path to the hermitage runs right past here, don't it? You're not out here late at night, like I am sometimes, checking up. You have no idea, what goes on, after dark in these parts."

"Did you actually see him with...her?"

"Can't see nothing in the dark. Only dancing flashlights. I'd hear her laugh. Not an innocent sort of laugh but...you know, kind of dirty and low... You can tell a lot from a laugh, sometimes. An older lady, experienced. Not some young thing." He paused. "I don't know who she was. Your boss would likely know..."

"Izzy?"

"Yeah, he and Lucian were drinking buddies. Somehow I got the impression...They *shared* her."

"Didn't need to know that." Emerick rolled his eyes.

"Though I don't know," Asaph continued, "how having a woman on the side would lead to his being dead. Unless he killed himself out of pure heartbreak...If she left him."

"Maybe she liked Izzy more."

"Speaking of your boss...watch out! Here he comes now."

And sure enough, Isidore was huffing up the path, in his work habit and brewers' apron, looking quite cross.

"Hey, kid! Get your lazy ass over to the cider barn and start hosing off them crates like I told you!" He called across the field, then turned to lumber back down.

"Great," Emerick muttered. "He's in fine fettle today."

"Probably a little too much imbibing last night. Yep, you see everything up here..."

Emerick jumped up and ran after his boss.

"Izzy, I got to ask you something."

"All you should be askin' is, 'what do I do now boss?' "

"Stop being ornery for a minute and just tell me something!"

Izzy stopped in his tracks and looked at Emerick wearily.

"Don't ask me no questions about Lucian! I'm grieving as bad as you. I'm sorry you had to find him like that, but let me tell you, he was just human. That's all, just a man. Not a saint, not the perfect monk, but a good, decent man, at heart. No reason for anyone to kill him. Every one of us has a dark side, you know. His...was pretty wide."

"Did he tell you that?"

"He didn't have to. I could tell. I can always tell. You, for instance. You got a *huge* dark side, only you keep it all tied up in that good-ol'-country-boy package. But you and I, we experienced the same kind of military hell, the kind that marks a man for life. Me, Iraq. You, Afghanistan. You don't walk away from that a whole person. I know you got mixed up with bad stuff, too, in the military. Drugs, like a lot of vets..."

"Just painkillers, okay? Not heroin, or meth, or any of that hard stuff—"

"The thing with painkillers is...you still need to take them even when the pain's gone away, am I right?"

"I'm done with all that. I don't even drink our cider. Don't need to be altering my reality anymore, not here..."

"But then, you're not really planning to stay here. Are you."

"Why do you say that?"

"A strong young handsome buck like you, what the hell are you *doing* here? Don't tell me you were 'called.' Your place is in the world, you need a good woman. You need to get off this mountain, get back out there. You only came here to escape for a little while. A lot of men do. And then, they go." He paused. "Like myself, for instance. Except I ended up staying on...and on... Inertia, I guess."

"You telling me you don't have a true vocation?"

Isidore stopped and paused for a moment. "You know, joining a monastery is like committing suicide in a way. Merton said that, in his writing. Leaving the world. But you still carry in all the same problems you had out there, they just kind of intensify here, sometimes."

"But you stayed."

"Well, I got things to do here, I've got a purpose, an occupation. It's not a bad life. And the spiritual life...it's there, in its own way..."

"You were going to tell me about Father Lucian. About his dark side."

"He never talked much about it. But we would get drunk together every now and then. You know that. He told me about growing up in a Catholic orphanage, never knowing his parents. Not the Philbertines, a less enlightened order. Wasn't pretty."

"Oh, God," Emerick murmured. "What did they do to him there?"

91

"He didn't say. Just hinted at it. Probably the usual emotional starvation, combined with beatings, molestation. He didn't come here to Skerritville till his forties…I guess he thought he was at peace with it all, finally, but he kept having flashbacks, nightmares. He was still feeling at odds with the Church. And yeah, so he acted out, now and then. The drinking, and…" Isidore looked about, as if to make sure they were alone and unheard.

"Yeah, I know. A woman. Who was she?"

"You wouldn't know her. A plant lady—horticulturalist. We had her up here to look at the orchard once, the soil and such. Teaches at the junior college in town. Know who her husband was? Still is, I guess. Doc Wheeler, who used to be the monastery physician. Marion couldn't stand working with him, though. Said he was a righteous know-it-all, and yeah, he could be. An honest doctor, though. Don't really think he was cheating us, like Marion said."

"Cheating us? How?"

"I don't know, something to do with Medicaid claims, insurance…Who knows anymore, with that stuff. But his wife…she sure was stuck, on Lucian."

"Wait, *I* went to Skerritt County College… for a little while. Don't recall any sexy older lady teachers though. But then I never took any horticulture courses."

"What did you study there, Theology?" Isidore snickered.

"Law enforcement, believe it or not. But back to this lady…"

"She wasn't that important. She wasn't that important, to *him*." Izzy said, with a shrug. "For him she was just…entertainment. I don't think she would have anything to do with him dying."

"He used to meet her at the hermitage?"

"Yup. I believe she was the one…who cut that hole in the fence, with a big old pair of wire clippers. Snuck in through the state forest."

"You ever meet with her, up there?" Emerick asked, looking his boss in the eye. "You can tell me, one Army man to another."

"Nah." Izzy looked away. "Wasn't my type. She was a...well, she was no good. Let's just leave it at that. Enough of this now, get back to work—" They were interrupted, when a group of men wearing working clothes and hard hats entered the orchard.

"Say," said their foreman, "Can either of you fellas direct us to this 'hermitage' trailer we're supposed to take down?"

"Well, speak of the devil-building," Emerick quipped. He pointed uphill. "Just follow that trail there, guys, you can't miss it."

Isidore looked startled. "They're taking down the *hermitage?*"

"Abbot's orders, but I didn't think he'd do it so soon. That reminds me, I have a phone call to make—" He pulled the cellphone from his pocket, and Isidore suddenly made a grab for it. Emerick jumped out of his way.

"Hey, gimme that back! You're only supposed to be borrowing it!"

"How'd you get one of these anyway?"

"Someone give it to me, that's all. I'm gonna to get rid of it, can't afford the fees on it no more..."

"Just give me a little more time, I'll return it. Took the charger out of your office. I just need to call my brother in Spitzville, and then...someone else..."

But a few hours later, during meditation and private prayer in his room, Emerick began idly scrolling down the Recent Calls list on Isidore's cellphone. He was startled to see a number of calls from a *Mary Weatherspoon*—including one made just a day before Lucian's death. *August 2.* He frowned at the name: Who *was* this woman? Was she the same Mary from Lucian's day calendar? His concubine? Out of curiosity, he punched at the number. After a few rings, a haughty but richly feminine voice answered.

93

"Izz-i-dore? What are you calling me for?! What the *hell* is going on at that unholy godforsaken place!"

Emerick swiftly ended the call. And paused to wonder, at the vehemently angry—and frightened—tone of the woman's voice. He stared at the phone a moment longer, wondering what else he might find out about Isidore, within the flat little cellphone. But he thought better of it, turned the phone off and returned to his spiritual reading.

Meanwhile, at the library, Callixtus was staring, in disbelief, at a written assessment test he had just given to Odo.

"You already *know* Latin. You seem to be fluent in it."

Odo nodded, in a casual way.

"Clearly, we've underestimated you. Nevertheless, you will still report to me for lessons." He spoke without looking at Odo. "I'll give you some of the more challenging Church texts to decipher. Go ahead, you can leave now." He glanced up. "Why are you limping? Is that...Is that *blood*, coming out of your foot? Your *bare* foot!" He jumped up from his desk and took Odo by the arm, practically dragging the young monk down the corridor toward the infirmary, leaving a trail of reddish heel marks behind.

Some time later, Brother Marion put down the surgical needle and thread he had just used on Odo's left heel, and gave the monk a stern look.

"Just because Brother Emerick goes barefoot doesn't mean you should follow his example! Philbertines wear shoes! There's a reason for that. You had the beginnings of a nasty little infection there. Might have to give you a course of amoxycillin."

Odo, sulking, turned away from him.

"Don't let that yokel fool you, he doesn't avoid footwear for spiritual reasons! He was caught by a bomb in Afghanistan—I think his boots melted to his feet or some such dreadful thing--then he developed a phobia about his feet. A kind of podiatric claustrophobia. It's purely psychological. But I am glad to have this opportunity to be with you, and get some general idea about your health. I understand you don't *talk*."

In response, Odo took his thick, nearly filled-up notebook out of his chest-flap, but was startled when Marion whipped it out of his hands.

"Okay, you're not going to be using this anymore. It's become a crutch, and you need to start using your vocal cords, because I assume you *can* speak, you simply choose not to. Probably psychological, like Brother Emerick's feet. Don't worry, in the meantime I have another tool for you, a better tool. We had a brother a while ago who passed on, he had suffered a stroke which took away his ability to communicate verbally with us." He rummaged in a cabinet, and pulled out what seemed to be a child's toy: A pale-blue plastic tablet with a screen and comically large keyboard, adorned with smiling whales and cheerful starfish. "Yes, it's made for a child, but you won't be using it long, just enough to help you transition into speech. This will make you understood by the other monks more readily. There are even emoticons here," he pointed to round keys with faces on them, "to indicate how you're feeling on a given day."

Odo punched the angry-faced emoticon key.

"Now, now, give it a try. If you don't like it, the alternative is *speaking*. Understand?" He took Odo's notebook and tossed it into the trash bin. "Come back to me when you need new batteries for it. You may go now, but I want to check on that foot in a few days. Go and put some shoes on, at once."

Odo stared dolefully at the tablet a while, then with a resigned gesture, slipped it into the chest-flap of his habit, then limped back down the hall in search of Emerick.

95

11.

A day later, Emerick himself changed Odo's foot bandage, gently dabbing the wound with disinfectant.

"Didn't mean for *you* to start going barefoot! I suppose Marion told you..." He looked up at Odo. "That my not wearing shoes is psychological. That's probably true. But it's also a spiritual thing. I like to feel the ground beneath my feet, in a *real* way. A connection to the earth, the world, I can't explain it. When you can feel the earth under your feet, you're...alive. When you can't, you're...well, *not*. The worst feeling in the world, was being in that explosion, when I went flying. I just lost contact with the earth and didn't know where I'd end up...And then I couldn't walk, for a long while. The best feeling...was to feel solid ground under me again. Never told anyone that before." He glanced up at Odo, in a self-conscious way. "But that's just me. Not you. Most people are meant to wear shoes, and probably you too."

Odo now took out the blue-plastic tablet and threw it, with a disgusted gesture, on the table beside them. Emerick sighed too when he saw it. "I can't believe he gave you that stupid *toy*. But you don't have to use it with me. No one should force you to talk before you're ready. But maybe you should use it for a while with the other monks, just to show Marion you're cooperating." He paused. "I think he thinks...I'm a bad influence on you."

At this Odo broke into a big grin.

"And I am, ain't I? Maggy says so too. But she don't mean it." Emerick laughed. "Here—" He gave Odo the coveted bright-red thongs he carried in his hip pocket. "Might be a little big for you. But I still got Gramma's flip-flops for when I need to be *calced*. Well, come on, we have someone to see. A visitor, who might be able to help us out with this whole money and Lucian thing."

Sheriff Ardelle was already in the visitor's parlor, when Emerick and Odo arrived. She was sitting at a small table with Brother Bart, sipping fragrant, amber tea from a delicate porcelain cup.

"Hey there, Biff. Thanks for calling me. Boy! I wish everybody greeted me so dignified and nice like this. Look, they've even got cookies. Pepperidge Farm. Very *posh*." She grinned.

"Good to see you, Dell. Knew the abbot wasn't going to call you, so I figured I better."

"What's this about? Something to do with Father Lucian?"

"Not really... Bart, this is kind of private and official, do you mind?"

"Aw, can't I stay, Biff? Already feel bad about missing your grandma."

"I don't think you should," Emerick told him, gently. "But maybe you should go and fetch the abbot for us."

When the old monk left, Emerick continued: "Odo and I found a huge pile of money here on monastery grounds. I mean, a lot. Like, thirteen thousand bucks. In a Publix shopping bag."

Ardelle paled slightly. "Omigod. That's *insane!* Where was it?"

Emerick picked up a Milano cookie and bit an end off it. "Brother Odo here found it in the hermitage, stuck under a bed mattress. I was with him."

"The herma-*what?*"

"Our prayer house. Or should I say, our prayer trailer. It's up on the mountain, about a quarter mile up from here. It's being dismantled, as we speak."

"*What?*" Ardelle jumped to her feet, just as the abbot was sweeping into the room. She leveled her charge right at him. "Why are you tearing that building down before I have a chance to search it?! It could be a *crime* scene!"

The abbot was almost too stunned to reply.

"Did...did... we have...an appointment, Madame?"

"Sheriff don't need no appointment, Mister! Let's get up to that hermitage—"

The abbot stiffened. "We do not allow women within the enclosure but—"

"You WILL be allowing this woman in," Ardelle snapped, slamming down her napkin. "Wait, wait, wait. Wait a minute. Before we go tramping up there. I want to see the *money*. You got it in a safe somewhere, Abbot?"

"In his office. Right behind ol' Saint Philbert," Emerick chimed in.

"Just a minute!" said Odrian, now entering the room. "Doesn't she need to present a search warrant, or something—"

"Father! We already told her about it!" Emerick scolded. "Are we *not* going to co-operate with the law?"

"Come into my office at once, Mademoiselle Sheriff," Dom Frederique said, with some unexpected graciousness. "In truth, I am glad you are here. The money has been weighing on my mind." He ushered her down the hall, and into his office, with the others following. He then went directly to the wall.

"Father Odrian, if you will..."

Once again, Odrian pushed the painting aside, holding it up with his shoulder while the abbot deftly entered the combination. He opened the door....then stood, looking inside with a stunned expression.

"It's gone! The money...she is gone!!"

Now they all rushed to the wall, craning to look inside the safe's interior, which was, indeed, completely empty.

Ardelle turned to Emerick with a deeply skeptical look.

"Biff..."

"I swear, we all saw the abbot put the money into the safe just last Friday!" Emerick exclaimed. "And he's the only one with the combination."

"Did you remove the money, sir?" Ardelle asked, in a low voice.

"*No!* I am as stunned as the others," the abbot murmured. He turned and looked at Emerick, then Odo, and then...at Odrian, who started.

"*I* don't have the combination! I never did!"

"This is impossible!" the abbot snapped. "*Someone* took the money from this safe!"

"Maybe a break-in," Emerick suggested. "That's an old safe, it mightn't take much to crack the combination. Except no one could get past Brother Bart—"

"Yeah, except when he's taking one of his half-dozen naps," Odrian remarked.

"Inside job," Ardelle murmured. Emerick gave her a worried look.

"Dell, I'm so sorry we brought you down here. I swear, there was thirteen thousand dollars in that safe. And the others can vouch for me."

"Well, I can file an official report of a robbery, I guess...But you boys are going to have to figure this one out yourself. If it turns up, be sure and give me a call."

While Ardelle stayed and filled out her report with the abbot, Emerick and Odo began to make their way down the corridor. Emerick paused for a moment.

"You didn't happen to—No, that's stupid! Why would *you* break into the safe and take that money?"

Odo's look of indignation shamed him.

"You're right, I'm sorry to have even thought—but you *are* good at breaking into things—"

"Emerick!" Odrian suddenly came rushing down the hallway after him. He actually grabbed Emerick by the arm, his forehead moist with sweat. "Do you think...do you think the *abbot* took it?"

"What? Why would he—"

"You know *I* didn't!"

"No one said you *did*, Father Odrian!"

"The thing is...we don't know him, do we? The abbot. He's new, he's...so different, than Dom Rasmus."

"Are you actually accusing *him*—"

"Well who knows, I'm saying we don't know him. He may have taken it and put it somewhere else. But what if the criminals come looking for it?!"

"Why are you so certain criminals are after us? Wouldn't they have shown up by now?"

"It has to be criminals! People from *outside*. Who among us in this community has thirteen thousand dollars?!"

"Monks collecting ginseng, maybe?" Emerick suggested, archly.

Odrian was nonplussed, for a moment. Then he scowled.

"There's no ginseng left to collect around here. It's all gone!"

"Are you saying that the monks collected it at one time, and sold it?"

"I don't know anything about that." And with that, he turned and trotted back to his office.

Emerick and Odo exchanged a look.

"It sure is a puzzle, isn't it?" Emerick jammed his hands into his hip pockets. "Well, I think I need to take a little trip into town. Do some research. You can't come with me, I gotta go *incognito*. Secret mission. Besides, I don't want to get you into any more trouble, with Marion or the so-called novice-master."

12.

Emerick stood alone by the edge of the road into town, a small distance from the monastery. It was mid-afternoon, the hours between dinner and Vespers, and Brother Isidore thought he was in the barn repairing some of the apple crates. But he was waiting for his brother, Gary to arrive. As he waited, and the wind whipped up the fabric of his robe, he found himself brooding over the missing money, and the weird handful of clues he'd turned up so far.

As soon as his brother's lime-yellow Chevy Sonic crested the hill, he pulled off his monk's habit, revealing clean and pressed khakis, a deep blue polo shirt—the very clothes he had worn the day he entered the abbey. He wore his Converse sneakers, and his feet felt positively claustrophobic inside them, his remaining toes squished to the limit.

He jumped into the passenger seat, throwing the robes in the back seat. Gary stared at him in astonishment.

"Go on, drive," Emerick snapped. "Skerritt County College, the west-side campus. What are you wearing that shirt for?" Gary was in torn-up blue jeans and a very old and faded 'Mountaineers' T-shirt.

"We're supposed to be landscapers! Isn't this how a landscaper would dress?"

"You didn't even go to WVU!"

"Well, I think it's fine! It's not like we're actually looking for advice on planting stuff, is it? What I don't understand is how you're gonna get this gal to talk about shacking up with your friend Lucian."

"I don't either," Emerick confessed. "But I can't meet up with her as a monk. Then likely she'd clam up and wouldn't tell me a thing."

"What do you think of all this, your fellow monks sleepin' around with ladies in town?"

"Not really in favor of it, if that's what you're asking. I can understand, though, how Lucian might falter. He's only human. I don't think the Almighty considers them love-sins as harshly as others, like murder or stealing. "

"You ever get the urge to…you know, sneak off…"

"I didn't take a vow of chastity," Emerick replied. "But I understand it as a sacrifice a religious man should make, has nothing to do with lovin' or hatin' women. It's pretty tough sometimes, but…you get through it…."

"Don't think I could," said Gary, in a faintly boastful way.

"Well, that don't make you any more of a man."

At Professor Weatherspoon's office, a hostile young receptionist tried to shoo them away.

"You have to make an appointment," she told them sternly. "Dr. Weatherspoon is a *very* busy lady. Leave your names, and I'll have her get back to you."

"No, we have to see her now," Emerick insisted. "We have a horticultural *emergency*."

The receptionist sighed, in a very put-out way.

"All right, go inside and wait for her. She'll be stopping by after class."

Inside her small, cramped office, Emerick discreetly looked about clues: He saw no evidence of Mary Weatherspoon's personal life: No photos, not even a diploma, only framed up vintage botanical prints on the wall, her desk filled with paperwork, monographs and horticultural trade publications. "Seems like a very serious lady," he murmured to his brother. He suddenly pointed to a small dish full of paperclips sitting on her desk: Mingled within was a single, pearl, earring.

"Bingo! The partner to the one I found at the hermitage, in the bedroom! Now I know I'm on the right track!"

"Wonder what she *looks* like?" said Gary. "Those older ladies can be *hot*. Cougars, they call them."

"What difference does that make?" Emerick snapped.

"Well, I don't know, but doesn't the kind of woman a guy is into say something about him?

"You dope." Emerick settled back into a chair. "Dear God, my feet are *killing* me!" he moaned, reaching to loosen the edge of his sneaker. "And these pants...I just can't get used to wearing to wearing them again, they're so confining! How can you stand it?"

"Are you *kidding* me? Wait--*shhhh*," From outside, they heard the receptionist complaining in an aggrieved way about the two visitors who "wouldn't go away."

"Gentlemen." The voice was clipped, impatient; the address, a faint reprimand. But at the same time, hers was the same deep, richly feminine voice Emerick had heard on the phone. They looked up and watched as Professor Mary Weatherspoon entered the room. She was as simple and practical as her office, a no-nonsense sort of woman, dressed in a blue chambray shirt and gray cotton slacks. She was neither slim nor plump, her graying brown hair cut in a simple frame around her slightly double-chinned face. Gary glanced toward his brother, his expression full of surprise and faint disappointment.

"Professor Weatherspoon," Emerick began. "Forgive us for...intruding..."

"Amber said something about a horticultural emergency?" She was not smiling.

"Well, not quite, we just—"

"Let me do the talking, Gary. You see, ma'am, we're the Ottelsby brothers, Gary and Biff, we're locals, and we've come up with a plan to start a commercial orchard outside town. Maybe grow some cider apples."

"To compete with the *monastery*?" She seemed faintly aghast. "Why would you do that?"

"Well… You can't have too much cider, can you? I know the monastery's cider is very popular—it *is* very good—but they're too small and can't keep up with demand. So we would just be like…supplementing the supply."

She folded her arms together. "So, your question for me is…"

"We were wondering…what's the best species of apple, in your opinion, for growing in this part of the state?"

"*That's* your horticultural emergency?"

"We need to get started right away!" Gary exclaimed. "It's August, already!"

Her hostility faded a bit. "Of course, you *would* want to get new trees in before the fall frost, though spring planting is really best, as I'm sure you know." She came around and sat behind her desk. "I have to tell you though, the monastery does have several *proprietary* apples. Unique hybrids of native trees and one from the Pyrenees region of France, and it needs a specific type of soil in order to thrive. I can make suggestions to you, but your soil would need to be tested first—"

In response, Emerick instantly produced a clear ziplock bag full of deep black loam and set it on her desk.

"Fine then. Leave that with Amber outside on your way out and she'll send it to the lab. We take checks or credit cards for payment. We'll get back to you via email with the results." She stood up. "Good day, gentlemen," she added, briskly, but with a polite smile.

"Wait," said Emerick, half out of his chair. "We have other questions, Professor. I mean, we came all the way down here because…well, our good friend, *Father Lucian Powers,* from the abbey specially recommended you, as an expert."

Her face froze.

"*Luke* spoke of me…to you?"

"Yes…ma'am." Emerick studied her closely, but could not see any additional clues in her face. "He spoke very high of you. He said—"

"He's *dead*," the woman whispered. "Didn't you know? He died, just last week. Surely you heard."

"What? Really?!" Gary exclaimed in an exaggerated way. Emerick dug an elbow into his ribs. "We *did* know," Emerick said. "I'm…we're so sorry, Missus Weatherspoon, I'm sure…You must have been *very* good friends with him."

The woman stood perfectly still for a moment, stoic. Then suddenly she raised her hands to her face and burst into ragged sobs. For a moment, Emerick lifted his arms, to comfort her, but then let his hands drop. He glanced at Gary as if to say, *what now?* and Gary shrugged.

"I'm sorry," she said, suddenly, roughly wiping the tears away. "I'm still in shock over it. Of course, the monastery is releasing no details. But they say he was found in the Heart-break Forest, where the suicides go. I can't believe…he would do that. He was completely against the whole idea of suicide! He was intensely…*pro-life*."

"I know!" Emerick exclaimed so vehemently, he earned a sharp look from the professor.

"How did *you* know him?" she demanded.

"Through…family… Our Gramma worked the gift shop up at Holy Face. We were both…baptized there, at the chapel. The old chapel."

"It's like our second home," Gary added.

"I see." She seemed to soften now. "You know then, that Luke was a good man. A *brilliant* man. Extraordinary."

"Yes. Yes, indeed." Emerick nodded solemnly.

"Were you *in love* with him?" Gary suddenly asked, sitting forward. Emerick groaned.

"What are you *doing*, asking a question straight out like that?" he hissed in Gary's ear.

"It's all right...Biff...I don't mind him asking. I don't mind admitting it. Now. I'm *proud* to. I did love Lucian Powers. I loved him with all my heart and all my being."

"Even though you're *married?*" Gary added. This time Emerick did not object; he was beginning to see a crude genius in Gary's line of questioning: Good cop, bad cop.

"I'm about to be...divorced," she said crisply. "I hear the disapproval in your voice. I'm not a Catholic, but I understand, there *is* something very wrong about a woman loving a man committed to celibacy. But I can assure you that our relationship was not *carnal.* It was an affair of the emotions and intellect, and the *soul.*"

"Yeah, right," Gary's voice dripped with skepticism. She glowered at him.

"It *was.*" She snapped. "It couldn't be anything but that... Not that it's any of your business! But our love was *chaste.*"

"Yes, ma'am," Emerick murmured, gazing at the single earring in the paper-clip bowl. He looked up at her. "Was he, like, terminally ill? Is that why he might have done himself in?"

"What? No!" she replied, at once. "He did have cancer, years ago, and treatment for it. As far as we knew, he was cured. It never recurred."

"Did he tell you that?"

"He didn't have to. He was not an invalid, or a sick man at all. He seemed to be in good health just before he died, in a good frame of mind, I can say that for sure."

"Mmm-hmm," Emerick murmured, under his breath.

"The thing of it is," the woman continued. "I was hoping, I thought I had just about convinced Luke to leave the monastery. To marry me. Spend the rest of his life with me, in godless bliss. But I think he needed to get used to the idea. And he wanted to finish his book. He said he was going to France, for good, but I believe eventually he would have come back, to be with me."

"Perhaps someone was trying to prevent that? Your...husband?"

"Oh no, I don't think so." She shook her head, with certainty. "It's true, we've grown apart these past years, hyper-involved in our professions. But my husband asked *me* for the divorce. You see, he has a bit of an infidelity problem as well, I've been putting up with it for years. For all his service to the community...he's also *serviced* a lot of the community. He isn't jealous, like that. He'd have no reason to kill Luke, if that's what you're implying." Her eyes narrowed. "Wait a moment...He didn't hire you fellows to investigate *me*, did he?"

"Why would he, if he doesn't care what you do?"

"Oh, because there's a lot of money, property involved. No children, but a big estate, houses, horses...You two *are* detectives! You must be the worst detectives in the universe but...Who hired you?" She moved a bit menacingly toward them both. "It's Hilbert, isn't it? He hired you, don't deny it!"

"Dr. Hilbert Wheeler, that's your husband, right?"

"You know that! How much is he paying you, to find out about me and Lucian?"

"Isn't he one of Gramma's doctors?" Gary asked.

"He wouldn't be working with your grandmother, I'm sure," said Dr. Weatherspoon. "Unless she's a drug addict."

"Well, you know," Gary added, "They say it's the husband who always turn out to be the culprits in these kinds of cases."

"My husband did not kill Luke. That's completely ludicrous. But I don't know who would. Luke had no enemies!"

"You really have no idea? Maybe one of the..." Emerick paused. "The monks?"

Her eyes widened. "Oh, *no*. Surely not! They're all such *good* men. Some of them are a little odd and strange, but... Well, you both say you know that place. Do you think any of them could be cold-blooded killers?"

Emerick and Gary answered at the same time. Emerick said "No," while Gary said, "Yes!" Emerick turned to his brother and fixed him with a cold stare.

"Hey, it's possible! A bunch of intense men, locked up together. In one way, none of them are suspects, but then, *everyone* is. When you think about it..." He wilted a bit, under Emerick's stare of disbelief.

"I didn't know many of the other monks. As a woman, I wasn't *technically* allowed to enter the monastery grounds. I would visit Lucian at this little trailer at the top of the mountain—I found a way to sneak in, the back way through the state forest. I did consult occasionally with Brother Isidore, the orchard manager. He and Luke were *very* good friends."

"They were?"

"They drank together." She rolled her eyes slightly. "Luke did have his vices. But they were also working together on a project of some kind. I didn't know much about it. Luke tended to...hold back, sometimes. But it wasn't anything evil or illegal, something to do with plants and herbs, some new kind of beverage—"

"*Philbertine* liqueur," Emerick murmured, without thinking. But Mary Weatherspoon had not heard him.

"Luke was the researcher, Isidore the product developer, that's all I know about it."

"Were any other monks involved in this project?"

"How would I know?" She turned thoughtful. "I suppose it has to be said, another monk could be responsible, those men, all of them, are such mysteries, but...I *doubt* it. To be honest, gentlemen, I think my poor Luke was done in by an interloper. An outsider. The woods up there are filled with oddballs wandering in from town.

Poachers. I think he simply took a walk in the wrong part of the woods, and ran into the wrong individual, at the wrong time…"

"Could be," Emerick muttered, softly. "but what kind of poachers, precisely?"

"Most of Stilton Mountain is state forest land. No one is permitted to take anything from there, but of course, people go up there all the time, to cut down trees, take firewood, shoot birds, hunt, collect rare plants, pull up ginseng roots—"

"Ginseng?"

"Oh, yes. It grows all over Appalachia, but it's become quite rare. And there's a particular and rare local species, found nowhere else, that's highly sought after. Supposedly with a greater strength than the other domestic ginseng. Not so much in use here, but in China, and the East, supposedly exporters will pay huge prices for it. The last stand, I believe, is on the mountain, in the state forest. But there's a very stiff fine, imprisonment, just for collecting it. I'm telling you boys that, because I don't like the gleam I see in your eye, Mr. Ottlesby."

Emerick started. "Oh, I'd never…But that could be it, couldn't it? Maybe Father Lucian went for a walk, since the forest is not so far from the monastery, and maybe he really had to think things over, so he went into the deep woods there, on Stilton Mountain, and ran smack into a band of poachers…Funny that they'd go to so much trouble, though," he continued, thoughtfully, "to make it look like a hanging suicide. Stringing him up like that—"

"Hanging?!" She jumped forward a bit. "Is *that* how he died?" Her hand went to her own throat. "Oh…Oh my…Well, that proves it. It *couldn't* have been suicide. He would never have done it *that* way!"

"Really? Did he tell you…how he might do it, if he did it?"

"We talked about death once. He said, if his cancer ever came back…he might consider it, but really, he was very much against the

109

whole idea of taking one's life—he felt you should live out every moment, to the very end. We owed it, he said, to our creator. But he understood why people were tempted. He'd said if it were up to him, he'd want a peaceful, dignified, painless death. Not suicide, but if he did...It would have to be some kind of overdose, opiates, for sure. Maybe carbon monoxide. He would never, ever, *hang* himself. That's so...primitive. *Brutal.* And he was neither a primitive nor brutal man." She now gazed at Emerick in a plaintive way. "Who would do something like that, to such a kind man? *Who?*"

"I don't know," Emerick replied, softly. "But if I find out, I will be sure to let you know..."

"No," she said, suddenly, her mood turning. "Don't come back here, either of you. Go ahead and make your report to Hilbert now, at the hospital. But be sure to tell him....I did not kill the man I *really* loved!" She paused. "I'd sooner kill *him!*"

Back in the car, Emerick stared straight through the windshield, as his brother started up the car. Gary turned to him. "Did you see how nervous she was? Calm and uppity on the outside, but the way she kept twisting her hands—"

"Well, she thought we were detectives, reporting to her husband."

"She had something to hide, I'm thinking. I don't think she was telling us the whole truth, about herself and Father Lucian."

"What else could she be hiding? They didn't have relations, she said."

"I think they did, and she just didn't want to say. The pearl earring in the bed, right?"

"Yeah, well...They may have simply shared a bed, without being intimate. People do."

"What was the project he was working on, with your boss?"

Emerick shook his head. "Oh, Izzy's been trying to invent this new liqueur, nothing secret or shady about that. I think it's idiotic, but he's entitled to try it. Surprised to hear Lucian had anything to do with it, but he does have access to research materials."

"Maybe he and Izzy had a fight—"

"We would know about it. You can't hide stuff like that in a little abbey like ours. The tension...you'd sense it after awhile."

"Maybe they got good at hiding it."

"Just drive, will you? I want you to stop at the hospital, though."

"You sick?"

"No! I just feel...I feel like I want to talk to Dr. Wheeler. Just to see if he knows anything..."

"Think he did it?"

"Don't think so, although he was the monastery's official physician at one time. He knew Lucian and had treated him. I really doubt he would have killed him, even if Lucian was sleeping with his wife. Doctors don't like to mess with their own work, I don't think. And if they were going through a bad divorce, why would he bother?"

"Know what, I just figured it out!" Gary hit the steering wheel with one hand. "*She* did it! The plant lady! She killed Father Lucian!"

"*What?!!*"

"I got it all figured out. I'll tell you what happened. She was crazy in love with him, right? And I don't believe that BS about it all being chaste! They *did* it, and did it and did it. The hubby catches her up there at the monastery, canoodling with him. And it turns out, that the husband really loves her, and is crazy with jealousy. And threatens to kill her. So, she goes to Lucian and says, now you have to marry me, protect me. But he suddenly says no, I don't really love you, never have, and she get all mad ..."

"And so, she strings him up in the middle of the forest, all by herself. Brilliant, Sherlock."

"Well, maybe her husband did it."

"That would make more sense than her doing it …I still don't think he did. I'm leaning toward that poacher theory. I just…I really want it to be someone on the outside, Gary. It can't be anyone at the abbey, it's just can't, I couldn't handle it, I…I'd *have* to leave. And I really thought the monastery was the place for me, a place of good, decent people. And peace. Lucian, of all people, told me it was. He can't be wrong. But now he's dead…maybe, because he *was* wrong."

Gary steered the car back onto the main road into town. "Say, how 'bout we stop at the Shake 'n Snack in town, for a quick burger and milkshake, before you go back to your dinner of bread and gruel, or whatever the hell you guys eat…"

"No, I need to go see Dr. Wheeler first."

"Okay. We could pretend to be detectives sent by his wife—"

"*No.* You know, you're enjoying this a little too much. Maybe this is *your* vocation calling you, big brother. Maybe you could go to private detective night school, or something."

"Yeah, well maybe *your* real calling is being a detective. Ever think of that? Hey, Biff—?"

Emerick was suddenly staring at something beyond the dashboard. "Pull over here, just for a minute."

"What? Why? Is my car making that noise again?"

"Look, over there. At the bank on the corner…That monk…the *abbot!* Dom Frederique, he's going into the bank. He's left the monastery, and he's here in town, in his robes and everything…" He turned to his brother, still seeming shocked at the sight of the abbot, in the grimy, slightly ramshackle downtown section of Skerritville. "Why is *he* going into the bank?"

"Why don't you go in and ask him?"

"We had a theft over the weekend, at the monastery. A huge amount of cash taken from the safe. And only he had the combination…"

"So go in, and confront him!"

"He doesn't know I snuck off monastery grounds! He'd throw me out for sure!"

"Isn't that what you really *want*?"

"No! I want...I just want to know what's going on. The money disappeared, and there's the abbot, going into the bank!"

"What money?! I can't keep up!"

"But... maybe the money's not connected with Lucian's death..."

"I don't know what the hell you're talking about!"

"Can't explain it to you right now... But just drive over to the hospital—next block. I'm going to talk to Dr. Wheeler ...alone." He reached into the back seat to grab his robes. "But no more subterfuge. I'm going to talk to him as myself.... as a monk of Holy Face Abbey."

Back at the monastery, Odo was flat on the floor of the main reception area, patiently scrubbing the grout between the massive blocks of slate with a toothbrush and lemon-scented Lysol. He wasn't sure why Brother Callixtus had assigned him this chore--which was related to the blood-stains his heel had left on the floor a few days earlier--only that it was some kind of penance. Either for falling asleep in his Latin class, or simply for being Brother Odo, and all the faults and inefficiencies connected to that.

He didn't really mind the labor, though. There was a strange sort of relief and even delight in seeing the gray grime and dark spots come up off the grout, revealing the grainy creaminess of color below; the scent of antiseptic citrus was bracing, and he was fascinated by the blocks of slate, precisely cut into squares and mined locally. Each piece was a different shade of gray-blue, each with its own, distinctive ripple pattern engraved into its surface. In one he actually detected the barely visible coil of an ancient snail, and he spent extra time with that square, tracing its pattern with his finger, trying to remember the exact name of it—he had always been fascinated by fossils and dinosaurs, and in Quebec, had spent hours gazing at the old books describing trilobites and ammonites and pterodactyls, trying to image a world before monasteries and people, marveling at the divine design of all of it.

As he worked, a few monks whizzed by, their robes flapping softly as they sped past him. He became aware, strangely, of their feet, realizing how unusual Brother Emerick's determined discalcement was. Virtually all of them wore shoes of the conventional type: brown or black, usually loafers, though the abbot—who had just left and locked up his office—wore freshly polished black wingtips. The outdoor monks, Odo recalled, usually wore ecclesiastical leather-strap sandals, not the bright-colored dollar-store flip-flops that he and Emerick favored.

He wondered where Emerick was. He had not seen him since morning liturgy, nor at mid-day meal. Usually he had a sense of where Emerick was, at any given moment, but now his mind simply went blank when he tried to think of him, and that concerned him a little. The abbot, too, had gone off somewhere, which was unusual since he usually stuck close to his office, and now he heard the quick, nervous patter of Father Odrian, the faint breeze of his robes as he swept past, pale-brown loafers paired with black compression socks, on his way to the back door. And he heard something else…

He rose up to his knees, as Odrian slipped out into the sunshine. He'd heard a faint rustle, like an autumn wind stirring up a pile of dead leaves.

Or, the sound of a plastic grocery bag, crinkling…

Rising from his work, he went to the door to look out, to see where Odrian was heading. He watched, a bit bewildered, as Odrian headed past the vegetable gardens, toward the orchard and the cider barn. He stepped outside a moment, intending to covertly follow him, when he suddenly felt his cowl being tugged from behind.

"Trying to escape your responsibilities, are you?" He heard the stentorian voice of Brother Callixtus behind him. "You need to discipline yourself, if you are to remain among us." He took Odo by the shoulders and forcibly turned him around. "You'll have your break at Vespers, with the other monks. Now get back to work, and put your very soul into it!" And with that, Callixtus promptly himself disappeared back down the other end of the hall.

Odo obediently returned to his bucket and toothbrush, but his mind abuzz with thoughts and ideas, the new puzzle of what Father Odrian may have been up to.

With a big plastic bag full of money stuffed in his habit...

13.

At Skerritville General Hospital, Emerick had little trouble getting in to see Dr. Hilbert Wheeler, who now spent more of his time in his office than on the wards, as head of the department of Community Addiction and Drug Abuse. His receptionist, who recognized the Philbertine habit, told him he could have a few moments with Dr. Wheeler, but only a few.

He paused, outside the waiting room of the drug-addiction treatment wing, shocked at the number of people he saw there. Men and women, young and old, they looked up at him in a faintly expectant way, as if he had something to offer them. *I was where you all are now*, he wanted to tell them, but wasn't sure what he would say next. Would they be too discouraged, if they knew how hard it was? He continued on to Dr. Wheeler's office.

Wheeler greeted him genially, but warned he really had little time to spare.

"Big problem in these parts, the drugs, addiction," said Wheeler, grimly. "But I always have time for one of the Philbertines. Still have a soft spot in my heart for you guys." Wheeler was a big man, slightly obese, balding, fiftyish, not exactly the image of a compulsive philanderer. "Tell me, have they gotten rid of that nutcase in the infirmary yet?"

"Nutcase? You mean…Brother *Marion?*"

"Yeah, that's the guy. Doctor Montgomery, Angel of Healing and Light." And he snickered, to underscore the fact he was being ironic. Emerick stared at him.

"Brother Marion isn't a doctor, exactly—"

"The hell he ain't. But he's not going to tell you guys that, is he? Your past in the world is the past, no one needs to know about it, right? I'm sure he's not telling y'all that he used to be a full MD, a practicing physician in the suburban Washington DC area. He lost his license to practice medicine…for over-medicating his patients, sometimes even killing them! Accidentally, he said, of course. There were lawsuits, bankruptcy. I guess the monastery was a convenient place for him to hide out in."

"Is that…is that *true?*"

"You could look it up, on the Internet. The Washington papers covered the trials, I'm sure."

Emerick placed a hand over his mouth and chin, to keep his jaw from dropping.

"I tried to warn the abbot about him, the old abbot. He died recently, didn't he?"

"Yeah, we have a new guy now." Emerick was still trying to digest this new information. "I didn't come here to talk about Brother Marion, but…Do you think he's *dangerous?*"

"I suppose that depends on your view of life and death in general."

"How do you mean?"

"Marion was a big proponent of eradicating pain. There was a kind of movement toward that, about a decade ago. Give patients all the medication they ask for, even if it poses a risk of addiction.

Enhance their quality of life, and that overrides any moral or ethical question about prescriptions, or the number you write out. Trouble is, it's all kind of backfired, and has led to the problems we're seeing today, particularly with the opiates. If you ask me..."

"So he felt...he was doing a good thing? Prescribing pain killers, relieving people of their misery..."

"Don't know what that man was really thinking. He's pretty smooth. I only know he got me out of the way pretty quick, he turned old Rasmus against me with some trumped-up charge of Medicare fraud, and I was forbidden to go up there anymore. So there's no real oversight over that man, I'm guessing. You don't have any other doctors going there, do you?"

"Come to think of it...no. He checks us out, gives us our physicals and such. Gets medicine for us if we need it..."

"I'm sure he does. What did you want to ask me about?"

"You heard about our brother Lucian, passing away?"

"Yes, the librarian." He shook his head, regretfully. "Good man. The radio report was very vague. Found him in the woods, did they?"

"Yes, it's a suspected suicide, but we feel...some of us feel...he was killed, intentionally."

"Oh, boy." Wheeler cast a worried glance at his desk.

"I'm sorry to bring this up, but it seems your wife was having some kind of...relationship with him."

"Yeah. She thought he'd leave the monastery for her. But if it wasn't him, she'd find another. She's a slut. Let me tell you this, and it's strictly confidential." Again he leaned forward, looking Emerick in the eye. "Pretty sure Lucian wasn't the only *monk* she was sleeping with."

Emerick nodded, sadly.

"She's a little sick, my wife. Doesn't have any faith of her own, wasn't raised with any religion, and yet she has a thing for religious men. I think it's the idea of luring, and corrupting, even conquering, a good man, she gets off on that. Hell, I'm no angel myself. I've had a few indiscretions …But at least that's kind of *normal*, for a man my age. Anyway, when the monastery contacted her to look over the orchard, it was like she hit the jackpot."

"Which other monks was she involved with? Do you know?"

Wheeler shrugged. "Don't know for sure. Don't want to sully anyone's name, and that's a matter for the confessional, isn't it? But I know there were others, I'm sure of it. She's a bit obsessive, my wife. That's why I'm divorcing her. She's trying to take the house, the beach cottage, the horse farm and racehorses from me, and I'm not rewarding her for bad behavior. Wish I did know the names of those other monks, I could use them in my suit against her." He glanced hopefully at Emerick. "Maybe you could find out for me, Brother. I'd appreciate it a great deal."

"Dr. Wheeler, I only want to find out who killed Father Lucian."

"And Marion hasn't been of any help to you on this? Seems to me, he of all people could give you a clue. Last to see the body, am I right?"

"He says its suicide, simple as that. He said Brother Lucian was terminally ill, with cancer. But you handled his case, years ago. Didn't the cancer go into remission?"

"Yes, as I recall. It was at a very early stage. And prostate cancer isn't as rampant as other cancers, there's a lot we can do with it now. But I hadn't seen Lucian in almost two years, so I couldn't tell you if it had come back, or not. Still, if Brother Marion said he was terminal and committed suicide as a consequence…I think you're very wise, to second-guess that opinion." He now looked at Emerick intently. "I think I remember you. Local boy, I knew your gramma, Beula. You entered the abbey just before I stopped going up there, but…combat veteran, weren't you? From the VA hospital in Virginia? Leg reconstruction?"

Emerick nodded.

118

"Had a bit of drug problem yourself, didn't you?"

"I did, but I was clean when I came to the monastery. Have been ever since."

"Don't let Marion give you anything. Come see me, if you have pain."

"All he ever gave me were those nicotine patches, to kick the smokin'. But...whatever he done in the past...I feel Marion is a good monk. I don't feel he would ever hurt anyone."

"Well, he hasn't hurt you, and that's a good thing..." He seemed to be thinking about something. "You seem to be doing quite well, perhaps that monastery's good for something, after all. But you do have some mighty strange men up there..."

At Compline that same evening, Emerick could not stop his eyes from flickering over the faces of his fellow monks, as they sang the psalm of the day and asked Virgin Mary for her intercession. His eyes went to Marion, who sat calmly across from him, his eyes fixed on his hymnal; beside him, in a wheelchair wrapped in blanket and still in his nightshirt, was one of the monks from the infirmary, the wood-wright Damascene, who seemed barely awake, silent but gazing with a startled expression at the stained glass behind the altar, his graying hair standing out in awkward angles to his head. Emerick glanced at the abbot, who looked dour as usual, a deep crease engraved into his forehead, the abbot he had seen whisking into the bank just earlier that afternoon. And then his eyes sought out Odo, who would certainly be expecting an explanation for his absence...but Odo was not in his newly assigned spot, on the other side of the altar.

Where had he gone?

After they proceeded from the chapel, Emerick broke ranks and went to go search for Odo. But as he did so, he felt a pluck on his sleeve. The abbot regarded him in a very stern way.

119

"Brother Emerick, would you mind telling me where you were this afternoon?"

"Well, Dom Frederique," Emerick replied boldly, "I could ask you the same thing!"

The abbot gave him a startled look, then turned angry-stern again. "Brother, come with me to my office. I think we must have another talk."

Odo felt intensely guilty about skipping Compline and Vigil, but he knew he needed to find out some kind of truth. As soon as the other monks filtered into chapel, he dashed out across the gardens and orchards, and ducked into the cider barn. He was surprised to find the hall with the inside offices unlocked. He suddenly felt a wave of guilt, for suspecting Father Odrian and the brewer for being involved in some kind of crime.

Who would leave a building containing thirteen thousand American dollars unlocked? Still, he had to check it out. For Emerick's sake.

He moved past the vats and cider presses, and the bottling room, into the corridor which contained Isidore's office. It was like a rat's nest of paper and bottles, beakers and pitchers, and even sticks and bits of dried plants, the exact opposite of Lucian's orderly library. He went to the desk, piled with books and paperwork, and tried to open one of the drawers. It was the exact same kind of desk Lucian had in his office, and locked up tight.

But…sticking out of the top of the bottom drawer was a tiny corner of beige plastic bag, something obviously thrown in, in a hurry.

Odo took out the little scissors he had purloined from Lucian's desk—he had become quite attached to them—and once again began working the lock with the tip of the blade, while mentally calculating how much time he had left: Compline took about twenty minutes, and it was already 7:15 pm and—

He suddenly heard footsteps making their way down the corridor. He pulled the scissors out of the lock, and jumped back.

"What the—What the hell you doing scuttling around in here?" But Brother Isidore didn't seem particularly angry, only curious. He even chuckled, at the sight of Odo. It was hard to be frightened of him, with his jolly face and big belly, shaking like Old Saint Nick's, but Odo was terrified. He quickly grabbed an empty wine bottle that had been sitting nearby, and mimed taking a swig from it, then gave Isidore an ingratiating grin. Isidore burst out laughing.

"Oho, needing a bit of Dutch courage, are ya? Don't blame you, the way that ass Callixtus has been riding you!" He sidled up to Odo. "You know he ain't really the novice master, don't you?" he asked in a low, deeply amused voice. Odo nodded.

"Have a seat, boy and we'll have a nip together, and no one will be the wiser. The old abbot, ol' Rasmus, he used to stop by evenings too for a quick snort before bedtime. Got something I want to try out with you..." He unlocked his desk and pulled a jug from a bottom drawer—a clear-glass jug with a screw-top lid, containing a strange, sludgy seaweed-green liquid.

"Of course, this stuff needs *years* to develop. This is a vintage from two years back. Take sip and tell me what you think. Well, you can't *tell* me, can you. I'll just go by the expression on your face!" Odo watched in faint horror as he poured out some of the contents into a paper cup, and handed it to him. He also poured out a dose for himself.

Odo stared at the swirling liquid in his cup. It was an intriguing color, shades of grass, sky, earth, sea...but as soon as he began to bring the cup closer to his lips, the scent of it made him gag: It was mostly weedy, grassy, but with nauseating hints of soil and manure.

121

"Go ahead! Don't sip it, just bolt it down, and let it warm you up from inside." Isidore himself took a swing, then smacked his lip, assessing it. "Seems to need something…"

Odo shut his eyes and swallowed a mouthful of the stuff. Almost immediately it came back up, and he ran down the corridor out into the open, so he could throw up into the bushes. Isidore's mocking laughter had followed him all the way down the hall.

14.

Emerick now sat with the abbot in his office, as the evening slowly began to wane into dusk. Dom Frederique sat stiffly on the other side of his desk, his hands together forming a kind of steeple. But he did not seem to be praying.

"Go on, Brother. I am waiting for your explanation about this afternoon."

"Dom, when I was in downtown Skerritville, about 3 o'clock pm, I saw you entering the downtown branch of Potomoc Highlands Trust…"

"And what possible business could this be of yours?"

In response, Emerick's eyes swiveled to the painting of Saint Philbert, then back to Frederique in an accusing way.

"Are you implying…Did you believe I was depositing the money I *stole* from the monastery vault?" The abbot was livid.

"I don't know what to think," Emerick said, helplessly. "How can that money be gone, when only *you* have the combination?"

"Brother, I went to the bank because the monastery maintains a safety deposit box there. In that box is another copy of the combination. I went there to *talk* with the bank officials to see if anyone had tried to access the box."

"And…?"

"Not that it's any of your concern, but *no*. No one has inquired about the box in years."

"Then maybe it was Father Odrian, impossible as that seems...given his skittery nature and all."

"One would think so, but I questioned him quite thoroughly. He denies going anywhere near the safe." The abbot sighed. "The bank manager suggested that if the safe were of a certain vintage, it might be very easy to break into it."

"Crack the safe? Yeah, it could be done by someone quick and nimble, but that person would have to know that the safe was here, and also that it was filled with cash."

"It is a mystery, just another in a series of unsolvable mysteries involving this abbey. Tell me now, Brother, why did you leave the monastery grounds this afternoon?"

"I had some errands to run in town..."

"Yes, well, you might have requested permission first. What sort of errands?"

"First, I went up to visit a horticulturalist, at Skerritt County College. Professor Mary Weatherspoon. She worked with Brother Isidore on the orchard, you know, apple problems and such."

"That seems reasonable. Did you have a particular problem you needed to discuss with her?"

"Yeah." Emerick folded his arms together, and looked up at the ceiling. "Turns out...She was *romantically* involved with Father Lucian."

"What do you mean, by romantically? Was it *sexual?*"

"Don't know for sure, actually. I'd rather not know. But they would meet up at the hermitage hut. Other monks saw them, but it was news to me, too."

Frederique wearily put a hand to his head. "*Mon Dieu*," he murmured.

"I though perhaps she could tell me something...Something that would prove that Lucian had been killed, and had not taken his own life."

"And did she?"

"Maybe. I don't know. I think she may have been lying. So I went to go see her husband."

"A jealous husband, perhaps....a suspect?" Frederique's weary anger had fallen away, and he now actually seemed interested in what Emerick had to say.

"Well, no, actually. The thing is, her husband used to be our abbey physician. Dr. Hilbert Wheeler. I say *was*, because apparently he had a falling out with Brother Marion and...oh, boy. Don't want to get into all that just yet but...He made me think that Marion might have drugged Lucian, either accidentally or on purpose, then made it look like suicide."

"*Why?*"

"That's the thing. The "why" of it doesn't make sense. He has no more motive than any other monk here. They got along, they seemed to like each other." He sighed. "There are too many threads to this. Too many stories. Too much *sin*, and shadow. It reflects badly on our abbey, and I understand now, why you were sent from France, to reform us. Kick our asses back in shape."

"I placed a long-distance call over the weekend, to the head of our order, to tell him of Lucian's death. Did you know it was Lucian himself who wrote to him, after your abbot Rasmus died, asking for a 'good man' to bring the monastery back under control? That is why I am here. Tell me, if you can remember, what happened when Dom Rasmus died. Not so long ago was it?"

"About two months ago, beginning of summer." Emerick paused for a while. "There was nothing suspicious about that, if that's where your line of thinking is going. He died at Skerritville General, after going to the ER with chest pains. He had heart disease for years, real bad. He died in the night. The next morning, at liturgy, Marion announced his death to us. He had gone in the ambulance with Dom Rasmus, and he told us that Rasmus had appointed *him* the new abbot. That gave us some pause, 'cause…usually we elect our own abbots. Frankly, I would have thought Lucian would be next in line, because of his education and experience."

"That is interesting. What did Lucian think of Marion appointing himself abbot?"

"He didn't say. He never spoke badly or judged any other monks. I did overhear him talking to Callixtus, right after we buried Dom Rasmus, he was saying something along the lines of, 'Well, let's just wait and see what happens next.'"

"Callixtus was upset, that Marion was abbot?"

"I think, in a sense, we all were. Not that we thought ill of Brother Marion, he seemed good and kind and fair, even if he is a little quick to dispense a pill or drug for whatever ails you. We knew he hated to see suffering. But…the way he stepped in like that seemed a little pushy, a mite, I don't know, arrogant. He's not even an ordained priest, but Marion said that in the Philbertine Rule, that didn't matter."

"He is wrong," said Frederique, grimly. "But go on."

"Brother Isidore, my boss, seemed to think it would all work out. He used to say Marion was a 'practical' man, and he wouldn't let things 'go to hell' like the old abbot did. What the abbey needed, he said, was increased revenue, and he thought Marion, along with Odrian, could do that."

"Odrian. Our nervous little sacristan and accountant."

"Yeah, Odrian had worked very closely with Dom Rasmus. He didn't seem very broken up about the abbot's death, but Izzy says Odrian has this kind of disorder, no empathy or sense of intuition about people—he's just afraid of them all. But he took up with Brother Marion as if nothing had happened.

"I gotta say, we did have these two weird sort of weeks after Dom Rasmus died, with everyone walking on eggshells and really practicing our silence, waiting for the next shoe to drop, so to speak. Which it did, when you showed up."

The abbot sat silent, thinking for a long moment. "Marion was... gracious to me when I arrived. Cool, but gracious. He immediately relinquished his post and went back to the infirmary. Well, he had no choice. What do you think were his true feelings?"

"Oh, I'm sure he was very surprised. Shocked even, that the Order stepped in. Maybe a little hurt or offended, that the Order didn't think him good enough to be abbot."

The abbot leaned over his desk. "Do you think...Marion is hiding something from us? Something to do with his...seizing control of the abbey?"

"Oh, I'm sure of it. But it's something he needs to admit to us himself. Trouble is, I don't know how to approach him about it."

"Here is an idea, Emerick. We will gather the monks together tomorrow in the evening, after Compline. It may be time to reinstitute the Chapter of Faults here, and discuss some things openly and honestly."

"Oh, boy, not sure that will work, Dom. Guys here can be real secretive."

"You can help me by opening it, being the first to speak."

"I'll do what I can."

"Meanwhile, I must commend your dedication to finding out the truth, even as we all tried to dissuade you. You have persuaded me that perhaps Father Lucian's death is worth looking into again. And the obscene amount of money you and Brother Odo found—now missing—must have something to do with it. You are a good detective."

"I'm not doing this for sport, sir, or out of curiosity." Emerick suddenly sat up urgently. "My own future at this monastery rides on the outcome of this…my faith, too. If Holy Face is not what I thought it was—how do I go on here? I came here, needy and hurting and wanting peace and God's good love, and for the most part I've found it but…who are these guys I live with, and trusted? My community, my family? I have to know, one way or the other. Is this a community that loves and protects its men—or destroys them?"

Frederique nodded solemnly. "Brother Emerick, I will support wholeheartedly your quest for the truth. But I implore you, no matter what the results, to stay here with us, to help bring the community back into grace and the sight of God. I cannot do it alone." He sat back. "Be careful! And know that I am here, for when you need me."

"Thank you, abbot." Emerick stood, then bowed to him before leaving, his heart feeling much lighter than it was when he entered. He left the monastery building and went into the front yard. The sun had fallen and the early evening was cool and a bit crisp, heralding the coming autumn season, which came early on their mountain. He came out just in time to see Odo hurrying down from the cider barn, with Erdwulf trotting behind him, and so darted up to greet them both.

"Hey, y'all! It's past both of your bedtimes! Where you been? What…what have you been eating! Some crazy color Popsicle?" He began chuckling. "Your mouth is all greenish blue!"

With a grimace, Odo pointed to the cider barn. Emerick laughed heartily.

"Oh, Izzy tried out some of his *Philbertine* on you! He does that to everyone—it's like your initiation rite! God-awful stuff, isn't it?"

Odo mimed retching, then shook his head violently.

"Well, I've just been with our new abbot," said Emerick, as they walked back toward the barn to put Erdwulf to bed. "He's a right, straight kind of guy I'm happy to say at last but…" He stopped in mid-field, to look Odo in the face. "Don't happen to know who was monkeying with his safe by any chance, do you?"

To his surprise, Odo pulled out his blue tablet and began pecking at it furiously.

I know! Followed by a shocked-looking emoji.

Emerick looked down, in the growing dark, at the screen, then up at Odo, peering into his eyes, trying hard to read the name that was in his brain. "O...D... Not *you*! Wait, *Odrian?*"

Odo nodded, then added on his pad: *he give $ to Br izidor!*

"Whoa. *Izzy?!!*" Shocked, Emerick looked over in the direction of the cidery. "Oh man. Oh man oh man." He rubbed his head. "Who's involved in all this? Odrian, Isidore, Marion....Callixtus? *Lucian?* " He turned back to Odo. "Does Izzy have the money with him now, do you know?"

in desk low drawer

Emerick glanced back at the cider barn, in an appraising way. "Okay. Won't confront him about it yet...let's see what happens at Chapter of Faults tomorrow night. That should be a very interesting get-together..."

15.

Later that same night—or extremely early the next day—while waiting for early morning Matins, Odo sat up in his bed, practicing English words on his baby tablet. He tried softly saying them, as the letters appeared on the screen. *Dog. Brother. Apple. Money...bag of money.*

Then he noticed something interesting, a button on the keyboard marked REC. Record? He pressed it and a little red light glowed.

"*Je... suis...* Odo...Leroi," he said softly toward the machine. He then pushed a button marked PL, and suddenly his own words, in his

128

own voice, came wandering back to him, sounding a little tinny and distant. He had never heard himself speak before, and now found himself marveling over the sound of his voice, breathy, hoarse and a little deeper than he expected. Not the voice of a child, but adult, even rather *manly*. It seemed faintly miraculous to him, and he felt he would have much to thank Our Lady for, when the monks met later in the night to sing to her.

At mid-morning, Emerick was in the kitchen, washing his hands at the big sink and getting ready to work in the orchard after morning liturgy, when Brother Bart came rushing in.

"There you are! You got a visitor, out in the parlor."

"Not expecting anyone. Who is it?"

"It's a *woman*. Didn't give her name."

"Ah-ha," muttered Brother Cook, his hands deep in a bowl of bread dough. "Brother Emerico has secret lover!"

"Not Ardelle, is it?"

"No!" Brother Bart gave him a look of stern disapproval. "One of them fancy rich ladies from town, up to no good."

Emerick swept into the visitor's parlor, where he saw, sitting primly in a corner of the room, in a funereal black suit, pearls and dowdy pumps, Professor Mary Weatherspoon. She gave him a stony sort of smile.

"Hello, *Biff*. Or it Father Biff?"

"Just Brother. Well, you caught me out. How did you figure it?" he asked.

"Hilbert told me he had a visitor from the monastery, just after you came to see me. I put two and two together. Is your partner Gary here, too?"

"No, just me. Look, I didn't feel I could approach you as a monk. But I needed to talk to you in a frank kind of way."

"Why are you after me, Brother? Did the monastery send you?"

129

"No. I just want to know who killed Father Lucian."

"Trust me, I had nothing to do with it."

"I might believe that. But you lied to me, about having a strictly chaste relationship with him, didn't you?"

"How dare you question that!" She was outraged.

Emerick dug into his hip pocket, where, among the other detritus and odd things he carried, he still had the pearl earring. He extracted it now, and dangled it in front of her. She reached for it, but Emerick closed his fist around it.

"Guess where I found it."

"Yeah, okay, in the bed, right?"

"Uh huh. What do you have to say for yourself now?"

"OK, it was sexual. *Sometimes*. He couldn't always…make it work, you know."

"And how many other monks were you sleeping with?"

"There were no other monks. Only Luke."

"You husband tells me otherwise."

"Oh, he's just making that up, to make me look worse than I am! There was only Luke, no one else. Others *wanted* to…but I only wanted Luke."

"So what brings you here to see me? Did you just want to let me know you figured out my game? You want your earring back?" He tossed it at her. "Or, just to let me know you're not a killer."

"*I* didn't kill him. But he surely was killed, wasn't he, and I'd like to know who did it, too. It seems to me you're well on the way to finding out."

"Don't know about that."

She began rummaging in her big, worn, leather briefcase. "I tracked you down because I got something in the mail, a small package. A clue, perhaps, although I don't know what it means…" She drew out a small parcel, its brown-paper-wrapping partly undone.

She pulled something from it and handed it to Emerick. "I think it came from *here*."

Enclosed in a plastic baggie was...a white-fiber knot. Emerick, awed, pulled it from the bag, and then held it next to the single knot on his own cord. Professor Weatherspoon leaned forward.

"So *that's* what it is."

"No note or letter with it?" he asked her.

"No. Evidently I'm supposed to know what it means. But I don't."

"It means...Can't be completely sure, but it means someone figured out you were messing around with Father Lucian in an unholy way. This represents his vow of chastity."

"It has to be another monk then!"

"Possibly." He took the parcel wrapping from her, carefully examining the label. It had been addressed to Prof. Mary Weatherspoon, in care of Skerritt County College.

"But...can't be from here, it's a computer-printed label, we have no computers or printers here."

"There's a UPS store just down the highway."

"Yeah but...most monks here wouldn't know that. You sure your husband didn't send you this? He might know, about the knots..."

"I don't know anymore. Am *I* in danger, Brother?"

"Might depend on how involved you were with Father Lucian. Did you have any kind of other project or arrangement with him? Any kind of business?"

"I'm a horticulturalist, he was a theologian, what kind of *business* would we be in together?" She shook her head. "It was why he said it couldn't work, we couldn't be...married." She looked mournful now. "He said, we could not be like normal people, living normal lives. And he said...even though he was a sinner, he could not ever stop being a priest, and monk."

"Yet, you couldn't leave him alone," Emerick said, in a slightly accusing way.

"I didn't chase after him, he called *me*, that last night—"

"That last night you saw him? That last night...before he *died*?" When she didn't answer, he continued: "You saw him the night he died?!"

"He was going to France. He was just about to leave. And he told me...he wasn't going to come back. He was going to stay there, at the motherhouse or whatever you call it, and be a good Philbertine. He said he couldn't do it here."

"You had a drink with him, up at the hermitage."

"Well, yes, but he'd had a few before I got there..."

"How was his mood?"

"He seemed fine. Very positive, he was almost *serene*. But that may have been the Scotch... He made his decision, he was ready to go..."

"You ended up in the bedroom, though."

The woman gave him a haughty glance. "Believe me, *nothing* happened. He'd taken his pain pills, and all that Scotch..."

"Then what did you do?"

"I left him, sound asleep. No point in dragging it out."

"And you didn't sense anything was...amiss? Was anyone else around?"

"No, I was... *distraught*. I didn't care if I was seen or not. I *loved* him! I didn't want him to go!"

"But he was probably going because of you!"

"No!" she snapped. "It wasn't me. It was *here*! This place! He needed to be away from here!"

"*Why?*"

"I don't *know*!" She stood up. "I don't even know why *I* came here! I just want to....." She turned to him. "Do you think I could...Could I at least just go, and see his grave?"

Emerick stared at her for a long moment. "I suppose…it's…it's not on consecrated ground. I'll take you there…"

He walked with her to the field by the edge of the woods, beyond the monks-yard gate. And stood silently, from a short distance, as Mary Weatherspoon knelt at the still-fresh wound in the earth, sobbing uncontrollably. Emerick felt a twinge of sympathy for her: He didn't doubt, now, that she had some real feelings for Lucian, whether they were reciprocated or not.

But as she passed by Emerick, on her way back to the parking lot, she lingered by him a while, and gave him a little half smile. "You might give me a call sometime, Brother…a nice sturdy boy like you, if you're having some issues, with your monasticism…"

And Brother Emerick was so stunned, he could say nothing in return.

16.

"Good evening, Brothers and Fathers," said Dom Frederique, as the entire non-infirmed population of Holy Face Abbey sat clustered in the refectory. "Tonight, we will be re-instituting that venerable and ancient practice known as the Chapter of Faults. This is not something you all should be dreading. It is my hope to bring a modern, very *positive* interpretation to it. Here is a safe place, where we can be open and honest with each ther, in confessing our own faults and transgressions, rather than accuse others, and so, seek a greater sense of community with each other. Who would like to begin? Brother Emerick, perhaps?"

Emerick, who had been sitting with his head resting on his hand, looked startled.

"Brother Emerick, you look like you have something to say," the abbot said, more emphatically.

"Oh, yeah. Well, um…to start with, the other day, Brother Callixtus here insulted me. He insulted me *gravely*. I was quite disturbed about it, but I have found it in my heart to forgive him."

Brother Callixtus, sitting directly across the table from him, simply lifted an eyebrow.

"How did he offend you?" the abbot asked.

"He called me… a *hillbilly*. You did, too, Marion. Don't know why you guys think that's okay. That's a slur, you know, in these parts."

Callixtus suddenly jumped up, as if he'd been equipped with a spring. "You ARE a hillbilly! You are stubborn, unschooled, un-*shoed*, pig-headed, under-educated, ungrammatical, and probably inbred; you personify virtually every tired, hackneyed cliché I have ever heard about Appalachian culture, including being related to every person in this one-horse town. That is not an insult, it's the *truth!*"

"Okay, I get it, you're still angry about Holy Thursday," said Emerick. "That was four months ago, so get over it. Besides, that wasn't my doing."

Brother Asaph chuckled. "Dom Rasmus made Clix wash Emerick's feet, during the Pascal Week Liturgy," he told the abbot. "Gotta say, it *was* pretty funny."

"A true test of humility, for Brother Callixtus," Marion said, with a little smile.

"Hey, he did a pretty good job, y'all," Emerick added. "Next year, I'm going to ask for a pedicure!"

"Enough!" Callixtus turned to the abbot. "There is nothing to laugh about here. You are looking for the dark cloud at Holy Face Monastery, there it is." He pointed at Emerick. "This man, this misfit, this so-called monk does not belong among us! I don't know how he passed his novitiate. He is delusional, disrespectful and perhaps even dangerous! Yes, everyone loves him, good ol' country boy Emerick! The prankster, the overgrown boy scout, the honorably wounded vet. And yet, who knows what *war crimes* and *atrocities* he committed, in combat, out on the field? Who knows how many Afghan babies he slew? Or women he raped? And he was a *drug addict*, into the bargain! Is this an edifying background for a holy monk of Saint Philbert? He soils the name of our order!"

The other monks, including the abbot, stared at him in shock. But Emerick calmly folded his hands together on the table.

"I wouldn't go there, dude. 'Cause Philbert was a soldier, too. Fought in the Crusades, remember. Soldier and monk. Father Lucian used to say that my life was following on the same...the same...*trajectory* as his.. If that's true, my spiritual epiphany is due any day now."

"You planning to start a new order?" Isidore grinned. "The Biffertines?"

"No, and not planning to get my guts ripped out by a team of horses, neither. And what's more, Clix, there was none of that atrocity stuff going on at my base. We weren't even engaged in combat, we got set upon by...a suicide bomber. A lot of good men died in that attack and why I didn't...tells me the Lord had somethin' in mind for me. As for my pain-pill addiction, heck, you'd probably develop one too if you nearly got your leg blown off. Still hurts when it rains."

Callixtus held out his hand. "And see how he does that, so effortlessly! So folksy and down to earth, making himself look like a modern saint and martyr, while I look like the Devil Incarnate, for daring to criticize him."

"Callixtus, I truly am sorry for making fun of you, and even baiting you sometimes, but you make it so easy, being so dramatic and overreacting and all."

"Really? Who is really the prince of drama here? You, with your absurd detective game of monastic Clue, trying to track down the alleged killer of a troubled man who clearly chose to end his own life…"

"He *was* killed, Clix. I'll figure it out, in a matter of time…"

"One can't help but think…you may be trying to deflect attention from *yourself.*"

Now Emerick could not contain himself. He leapt up and reached across table, grabbing Callixtus by the cowl, but several other monks jumped up and pulled him back, prying his fingers off Callixtus' habit. Callixtus, brushing himself off in a panic, gaped at the abbot in a horrified, but vindicated way.

"Wasn't going to *hit* him!" Emerick shook off the other monks, in an irritated way. "I was just trying to get his attention. I wanted him to look me right in the *eye* and say that!"

The abbot glared at him. "Is this a grade-school playground?! Are you six years old?!" he thundered at Emerick. "You will spend the remainder of free time this evening in the chapel, doing penance, and thinking about your actions. Brother Callixtus! You will join him, and think about your words. Enough of this absurd sibling rivalry, please, we have more important things to discuss!"

"And that is *exactly* what it is, Abbot." Brother Marion drew himself up. "Two brothers, competing for the attention of the father. The brothers being Callixtus and Emerick of course, the older one brilliant but emotionally needy and perpetually insecure, the younger spoiled, undisciplined and constantly seeking attention. The father, being the cunning Father Lucian. Who was not beyond playing them off each other, perhaps for his own amusement."

The abbot regarded him with some interest. "So this was noticed, by the rest of the monastery?"

"Of course. We're not supposed to notice such things, but we do. It's what serves as entertainment most days. Brother Callixtus would not have killed Father Lucian; he likely would have killed Emerick instead. If he were in that frame of mind…Although, after seeing

Brother Emerick lunge at Brother Callixtus like that…I'm worried that it's all grown out of control. Of course, Emerick is obviously suffering from long-term repressed PTSD, but Callixtus' demeanor gives me concern as well. Perhaps it's a blessing Lucian is gone now. But I would urge these two young men to reflect on their behavior and their relationship to the man each called their mentor."

Callixtus regarded him with a stony face, but Emerick…Emerick was smiling a little, almost as if he had just decided on his next chess move. "Well, go on then, Brother Marion! Tell us more."

Marion continued, undeterred. "Callixtus is right, we don't know much about Brother Emerick's experiences with the armed forces in Afghanistan—Kandahar Province, wasn't it? Bombing victims often suffer the worst trauma of all, because of the randomness, the suddenness of the event. And for him, alas, the trauma continued, during all those surgeries and the extensive reconstruction his leg needed, which in turn led to a serious reliance on opiates such as Percocet and oxycodone. Father Lucian's death was, in effect, a second 'suicide bombing', if you will. We know you're not violent, Emerick, but it *does* seem to me that this obsession you have with tracking down a mythical killer is the manifestation of some unresolved trauma from your wartime experience. You have come to see everyone as an enemy, even all of us, your own fellow monks." He delivered these words in a kind voice, and a smile. Emerick scowled.

"That's not true, Marion. I never *wanted* to think one of us killed Lucian."

"But you think…one of us did?" This was Asaph, in a worried voice.

Emerick shook his head. "No! None of us had a good motive or reason for killing Father Lucian. Except…well, Brother Callixtus."

"You did move in pretty quick to take over the library," Brother Isidore snarled now, throwing a pointed look at Callixtus, who looked horrified.

"Of course I wanted that job! But I would never *kill* for it!" He turned to Emerick. "Am *I* your number-one suspect now?"

"Oh, don't flatter yourself," said Emerick, rocking back on his chair. "If you think about it logically...You're right, you wouldn't kill for a position in this abbey, no monk here would. That goes against everything we believe. And I know how devoted you were to Lucian. You were a big help to him, translating all those Philbert documents for him, and really, you had no reason to kill him. Did you now."

Callixtus seemed somewhat appeased by this. "Then I say, continue your fruitless quest, if that is what helps you find peace, Brother. If that's how you have to deal with it, so be it. I suppose it's harmless..."

"I can't agree, Brother." This was Marion, again. "I think Brother Emerick's private delusion could prove harmful not only to himself, but to the monastery as well. If I were abbot, I would order him to stop, at once."

"Well, you were abbot once, Marion," said Emerick, quietly. "Very briefly. Trouble is, you didn't really tell us the truth about yourself, when you took over, did you."

The infirmarian was only slightly taken aback. "What do you mean by that, Brother Emerick?"

"Well, let me tell a story I heard about you, Marion. And it's the truth, Brother--excuse me, *Doctor* Craig J. Montgomery MD. Stripped of your license to practice medicine in the state of Maryland, for overdosing your patients, and *killing* one; abandoning your poor wife, and *children*, to come hide out here, among us, and start a new life? Don't tell me it isn't true, because I looked it up on the Internet." He held up the smartphone he was carrying all the time now.

"Hey! Give that back to me!" Isidore snapped. "It ain't yours!"

But at the end of the refectory table, Marion's face had turned a distinct shade of pale. Even Callixtus craned his neck to gape at him. The abbot, at the other end of the table, gazed down sternly as well.

"Hoo-whee, this Chapter of Faults is turning into a regular soap opera!" Brother Bart crowed.

"How could we not know this?" Asaph asked, aghast.

" 'Cuz Marion cooked up a deal with old Dom Rasmus," Emerick replied. "And I guess the rest of us were pretty much clueless. But none of us, really, have past lives that are open books. Well, except me, you can just go into town and ask anyone about ol' Biff. But we didn't know anything about you, for example, or even Clix here. We don't even know anything about our own new abbot, but we have to trust he'll be good for us. And we all trusted you, Marion, but it's like you kinda lied to us..."

Marion turned to the abbot. "This charge is not... *precisely* true. I *chose* to stop working as a physician. I was involved in a difficult case, involving the use of merciful pain medication. I did not even administer the final dose—the nurse in my charge took it upon herself to increase the amount. And the patient died. I was tried, but *not* convicted. The legal costs bankrupted me. I felt...spiritually bankrupted, as well. As for my wife...that marriage was *annulled*."

"With children?" The abbot raised his eyebrows.

"Regrettably, yes. My vocation came...in a roundabout way. But I have brought to it a significant amount of life experience, which can't help but be a benefit to my fellow monks."

"Did you indeed explain all this to Dom Rasmus, when you first entered the monastery?"

"Of course! He had heard about the case. But he was most kind to me; he said there was no reason any of the other monks needed to know about my background. Of course, he was in urgent need of a medical professional here. He told me, and rightly so, I would find my redemption here. And I have. Working here at Holy Face represents the best years of my life. I've been fighting to keep this place going, and support all these good men here, too." He turned to face Emerick. "Obviously in the course of your so-called investigation…You've been talking, no doubt, to people in town, a certain Dr. Wheeler, I suppose? Do you know he was overcharging us, and double-billing on Medicaid?"

"But…Doc Wheeler was a good man, he helped many of us," Bart offered. "He worked with us for years. So what if he got a little more than his share? He cured Lucian of the cancer."

"Yes, well, we don't know that for sure," Marion replied. "He never went back for his checkups."

"Say what you will about Wheeler," said Emerick. "He does good work for the poor folk in town now, addicted to drugs and such. So many people here, addicted…Why is that? Marion, why do you think it's such a problem here?"

"You ask that as if I had something to do with it."

"Just looking for your take on it."

"It's a problem everywhere. All over West Virginia, Appalachia, the Midwest…"

"I don't remember it being such a problem in Skerritville before. Seems to be specifically opiates, pain drugs."

"Easier to get," Marion responded, crisply. "Look, my only concern is this abbey. I cannot help the town of Skerritville, or the entire state of West Virginia. Only this abbey. And my life is here now, but still built around using medicine in the proper, most important way, the way it was meant to be used, to minister to my patients in a merciful way, easing their pain without incapacitation—"

"Like the fellows in the infirmary? Maybe you give them… a little too much mercifulness?'"

"What are you implying, Emerick? That I'm being careless? Unethical, somehow? *Immoral?*"

Emerick put his head in his hands. "No... I know ... I know you're a good infirmarian, Marion, despite all you've hidden from us. For the most part, you've taken very good care of us. I'm just...trying to figure things out. Something is very wrong here, something which led to poor Lucian being killed, and I'm just trying to piece it all together—"

"It's your own obsession. There is nothing wrong with our monastery, there is no darkness or evil here. But you suspect so, because there's something wrong..." He leaned up the table to give Emerick a long hard look, "with your *brain.*"

"Well, my brain did not conjure up thirteen thousand dollars, which Odo and I found up at the hermitage last week. Money the abbot put in his safe, and now it's gone!" He hit his fist on the table. "There, it's out in the open now! That's what this meeting is *really* about, folks."

Now truly nonplussed, Marion sat back. "I don't know anything about *that.*"

"Then who does?" the abbot shouted. "Those of you who used the hermitage in the past...why was that money there, and where is it now?! Who has taken it from my office? It may be an intruder from outside...but I need to know, now, if any of our monks are involved in some kind of illegal activity. This cannot be allowed to exist!"

Brother Callixtus sat looking slightly stunned, then glancing about in a questioning way at his fellow monks. Emerick's eyes went next to Odrian—who merely seemed nervous and panicky as ever, quivering a bit in his seat on the right-hand side of the abbot—and then to his own supervisor, Izzy, who sat perfectly still, even looking a little bored. Emerick didn't feel he had enough to go on yet, to openly accuse them; he found himself mentally willing them to speak, to own up. But the room remained silent, but for the buzzing insects and crickets of late August, filtering in from outside.

"Yes. I see," said Dom Frederique, at length. "This is perhaps not the right approach. Then we will be more private about it. Any of you may come and see me, alone, to discuss any information you have regarding this matter. You may see me, or, if you feel more comfortable, you may approach Father Odrian."

"But you should tell the abbot, though," Odrian added, quickly. "Not me." He jumped up and left the table, before any of the others.

After the meeting, Emerick remained at the table, with Odo, Bart, Christoph, and Asaph.

"Sure would like to have seen you whup Brother Clix," Bart said, a bit regretfully.

"Aw, didn't wanna do that." Emerick sat with his chin resting on his hand, feeling a bit dejected and also flummoxed, that the Chapter had revealed no significant or conclusive insights.

Isidore the brewer suddenly wandered back to the table. "What's this, a meeting of the Monastic Hillbilly committee," Isidore quipped. "Four true-blue Appalachians, and two honorary members—I think that's enough for a quorum."

"Don't got nothing to vote on," Emerick murmured.

"Don't we?" Isidore snapped back, and his voice had an edge to it. "How 'bout we vote you stop this nonsense about Lucian being murdered?"

Emerick's head shot up in surprise. "You takin' Marion's side?"

"I mean it, Biff. I'm not talking to you as a fellow monk, but as your boss. I let you go on awhile with it, but it's got to stop now."

"You ain't my real boss," Emerick snapped back. "Abbot is, and when he tells me to give up, I will."

"Yeah well, that new abbot, he's an outsider, he don't know nothing about nothing, but I'll tell you right now, going outside the monastery, like you been doing, spreading tales about murder and such...You are going to bring us all down, boy. It's already begun, maybe can't be stopped. The end of the world is coming," Isidore thundered. "The end of our world. Mark my words, next year this time, there won't be any Holy Face Monastery anymore. No more hard cider."

The other monks, including Odo, stared at Isidore in alarm, but Emerick scowled.

"What are you nattering about? You been drinking too much of that green swill you call Philbertine. That stuff is, by the way, a true *sacrilege*."

"Yeah, boy, go ahead and make jokes. How do you think we survive? Do you really think it's all apples and cider? Hell, we *lose* money making that stuff!" He went to the table now, leaning against it and into Emerick's face. "It's *donations*, you idiot, donations from the community, that's the only thing left now!" He pulled back a little. "Yeah, in the old days it was the ginseng. But that's all gone now. All gone." He paused. "You think people round here are gonna keep sending money our way, if they think something funny's going on up here?"

"Is that what that money in the hermitage was, a *donation*? A donation stuck under a bed mattress?!" Emerick countered.

Isidore went on, ignoring him. "The abbey can't survive this. And when Dom Fred sends word back to the big house in France…they'll shut us down for good. And that's all on you, boy. All on you."

Emerick stood up. "I'm going to do my penance now. And I'll be sure to particularly pray for your wretched old soul, boss. 'Cause I have a feeling, you're gonna need it."

After both he and Isidore went their separate ways, the remaining four sat quietly for a moment, sadly reflecting.

"He may be right," Asaph murmured. "Izzy, I mean. Much as I want to support Emerick…this could be bad. Real bad, for the abbey."

Bart eyed him sharply. "Biff's a good boy, he's smart, knows what he's doing. I tell you, he's gonna be abbot one day."

"That's a real exercise in faith, brother. If you believe that…"

Brother Christoph, who had remained quiet the whole time, gazing dolefully at the other monks, now stood and wordlessly left the room.

As did Odo, tucking his baby-blue tablet into the chest-fold of his scapular, in a very purposeful way.

17.

Odo made his way back to the cider barn, following Brother Isidore. He checked first to see that Erdwulf was curled up in his dog-bed for the night, amid the cider barrels, and then peeked into Isidore's office. As he had guessed, Isidore was settling in for a nightcap. He watched for a moment as the brewer pulled out a bottle of brown-amber liquid, taking a quick swig from it without benefit of a glass. He then entered shyly, and sat down at Isidore's desk. Izzy looked at him in surprise.

"What are you doing back here, kid? You want more of the green stuff?"

In response, Odo shook his head, and pointed to the amber liquid.

"Oh, the good stuff, eh? Yeah, I'd say this is a good night for a stiff drink. The beginning of the end…" He poured out a small portion of the Scotch for Odo, using the same—unwashed—glass he'd used for the Philbertine; Odo meanwhile, pulled out his toy tablet and began typing on it. *You can talk. I listen.* He held up the tablet to Isidore, but as he did so, discreetly pressed the REC button.

"Oh boy, Od-dee-oh." He gazed dolefully at Odo's screen. "I do need to talk. This poison, inside me, it's eating me up…Yeah, listening, that's a skill. It's all you can do, isn't it. Not like you can tell

144

anyone what I say, can you? You ain't going to run back and tell your old friend Biff, are you, whatever I tell you--In strictest confidence, mind you."

Odo nodded.

" 'Cause there's a lot here at the monastery Biff don't know about. I never clued him in on it. I wanted to protect him, like. But also, I thought he was...well, let's just say I severely underestimated him. He came here as a simple laborer, all shell-shocked from the war. Just got off the drugs. Who knew he'd turn into a half-way decent monk? Maybe there's hope for that Christoph boy, too."

Odo nodded again, rather emphatically.

"Lucian and I ran the ginseng operation together, and it was all above board, honest, profitable—great while it lasted. But of course it couldn't last. But we got used to that easy money. Me, Lucian, and our weaselly sacristan, Odrian. It was really how Odrian became our official accountant, because before that, we didn't have enough money to count.

"But let me tell you about Lucian. You couldn't help loving the guy, he was a warm and funny, great to be around. A real guy, a man's man. Genuine. And brilliant—should have been a Jesuit. He *believed*, he really believed and he could hold up those beliefs, in any argument against any unbeliever, and that was the only side most monks saw. But he couldn't *live* it. He had issues, he drank, he couldn't keep the chastity, but he was kind of trapped...he had no family, no where else to go. He wanted to stay here—he called this place Hard-Cider Abbey, and he loved the whole package, the apples, the mountains, the culture, even the people here. He wanted to keep it alive. But we needed money.

"So he did some research, got involved with the horticultural lady, and we tried experimenting with cannabis, but that was too expensive, needing greenhouses and all. So we tried looking into other forms of alcohol to sell. Thought I was on to something with the liqueur. But then Marion showed up. Guess that was about five or six years ago. He didn't tell us about being a doctor, but Lucian found out about it, somehow, maybe through Doc Wheeler in town. That was about the time Lucian was being treated for the cancer.

"Marion laid low for a while, but then Lucian had an idea. Marion may have been a disgraced doctor, he said, but maybe he could use his experience and skills for good. We began to talk to the old abbot about setting up a kind of retreat center, for people suffering from pain. A kind of St. Jude's, except for grown-ups. Palliative care, Marion called it. It started, see, as a *good* thing; that was all Lucian meant it to be. A way to continue as good monks, and provide a mercy and help for others. But Marion went and corrupted it all; Marion, and Odrian, got greedy. Not us."

"Marion had bigger plans for the monastery. He thought we could turn it into some kind of 'wellness' center for anyone, like a kind of spa, like the ones just to the east of here. People come out here for that kind of thing. He seemed to think the property here was worth a lot, and he said a 'spiritual spa' could make big money drawing in burnt-out professionals from Washington and even New York or New Jersey. He thought we could find investors—he even had Odrian look into it—and maybe even mortgage the property, but he thought we should try to develop it on our own first. But of course you need big money for that.

"I remember when he finally says to me, 'More revenue? Well, the answer's right there, over in the forest, isn't it?' "

Odo furrowed his brow.

Izzy leaned forward, his breath recking of Scotch. "The *druggies.* Marion still had connections, and he knew how to work the system, the drugstore chains and supplier. But Marion had a twist on it: We wouldn't sell the out-and-out get-high *bad* drugs, like heroin or meth, mind you. Marion insisted, if we were going the sell them, they had to be beneficial in some way. Pain relievers, but also cannabis and hash,

146

anti-anxiety meds, and the drugs you need to take to get off the bad stuff. No prescriptions, just cash and carry. He recruited several go-betweens, so we didn't have to go out there ourselves. Yeah, that weird kid, Christoph was one of them. A local, with a bit of a problem himself; that's how Marion kept him under control. Eventually we realized, though, that we weren't going to make a killing among poor addicts in the forest. We'd have to go head-to-head, with the street sellers in town and around the county."

"That's when Lucian backed out. He hated the whole idea of the wellness center, which he said would destroy the character of the abbey. The ginseng was one thing, he said. I'm not getting involved in this drug trade, this is immoral, unethical, he got all...as Biff would say, *biggity* about it. But he knew if he went to the abbot, and spilled the beans, that would be the end of it all, the good Scotch and the new books for the library and the trips to France and even basic necessities like food and medicine and our habits. We had just started working to get WiFi and computers in...So we told him to just step away from it, not to worry anymore, just let us conduct our business. I had my doubts too, but...You know, business is business. I've never been the idealist. And it was a business, just like the cider. You think we could meet expenses just selling that swill? And the business really took off, especially when Marion charmed our friend Mary into 'getting clients' for us, all those rich, hurtin' lady friends of hers, plus a bunch of her hubby's clients. A few pills, some spiritual advice in exchange for a big ol' donation...Marion saw it all as a kind of beginning for his 'healing' spa; he saw nothing wrong in any of it. 'This is the path for monasticism in the 21st century' he would say. Can't survive otherwise, he'd say."

Now Isidore paused, with a baffled expression on his face. "Didn't think Marion would *kill* Lucian, though."

At this point, Odo dropped his tablet on the floor; it landed with a loud clatter. He scrambled to pick it up, punching the REC light again.

"Not that I know that for sure," Isidore went on. "I just assume so. It was the very first thing I thought, when we heard Lucian was found dead. I knew he didn't commit suicide, he never would have. But he was threatening to expose the whole thing. So it *must* have been Marion, using some sneaky kind of drug, then setting it all up." He leaned closer to Odo. "Emerick needs to stay away from Marion, you hear? You can't warn him, but…just keep him away from that infirmary somehow. That boy's a pest and a fool sometimes, but he's good at heart and has a lot of living ahead of him. Don't want to see no harm come to him."

They heard footsteps in the hall leading to the brewer's office. Odo hit the record button one more time as Emerick burst into the room.

"Hey, what's going on!"

Isidore sat back. "Wasn't much of a penance you did there."

"Well, Clix never came in to do his, so I figured why should I. Odo, what are you doing here?"

In response, the younger monk jumped up and ran out of the office. Emerick turned now, as if to confront Isidore, staring hard at him for a long moment. Isidore raised a glass of Scotch to him.

"Well come on, boy. Join me for a drink. A drink to end-times, the end of the glorious experiment that was Hard Cider Abbey."

Emerick turned without a word and walked out of the cider barn. Then ran to catch up with Odo, as the sky darkened into night, and the green lightning beetles began to glow.

Just outside the door to the monastery building, Odo was frantically pushing buttons on his tablet. Emerick came up alongside him.

"What is it, Odo? What did he say? He didn't threaten you, did he?"

Odo was visibly upset: He had just realized that every time he hit the REC button, it erased whatever was recorded just before. The only thing he managed to record was Emerick's entrance into Izzy's office. He now began writhing and shaking his head, and grunting, as if trying to say something, something inexpressible—

Emerick took him by the shoulders. "What is it? What..." He now took Odo's head in his hands, and looked straight into his eyes. "I'm trying to...Trying to understand, but I can't, I can't...Your brain is too *full*. So many words, but I can't...I can't make any of them out."

Odo shook free of him, in utter despair.

"It's okay. Just be calm... Just go sit in the chapel a bit, and meditate. Then you find a piece of paper and pencil, and just write it all down, better to have it in writing, whatever you heard. But I'm positive now, Izzy is up to his neck in it...Did he say anything about Father Lucian?"

Odo opened his mouth to speak, but could not force the word, the name out; it would not leave his throat, where it sat, stuck and burning. He pressed his lips together. "M-m-m-m- Maaaa..."

Emerick watched him closely, unconsciously mimicking him. "Mmm...Mary? *Marion?*"

At the same time, something appeared in their peripheral vision: A light, bouncing off the fields just beyond. It swung round toward the monastery, briefly sweeping over Emerick's face, then back to the field. They squinted at the robed figure walking by in the moonlight, uphill toward the orchard.

"Christoph," Emerick murmured, recognizing his height and girth. "Where's he going?! Sneaking into town? He's going the wrong way...Toward the state forest." He turned to Odo. "I'm gonna follow him a bit—"

Odo grabbed his arm, in alarm. Emerick gently shook it off.

"I'll be all right, just want to see what he's up to…He's headed for the old hermitage, but that ain't there anymore. Don't worry—just go to chapel now and then to sleep, and we'll talk in the morning."

But Odo did not go in right away, but stood rooted to the spot, watching as Emerick made his way along the path up the hill. There was a near-full moon that night, which illuminated Emerick's flowing pale robes. He seemed, to Odo, to have been transformed into a ghostly angel, no longer something connected to earth but ready to disappear into the darkness and night air. He waited until Emerick had disappeared completely from sight, and then made up his mind to follow him—

But someone laid a hand on his arm. "You should go in now, son, the night air will give you a chill." The iron grip seemed that of the novice-master, but it was Brother Marion, the infirmarian, his voice deep, warm, soothing. "Go inside, and get some sleep." He actually pushed Odo, a little, toward the door.

Reluctantly, Odo turned and went back inside the monastery. He did not go to the chapel, but to his little room, where he laid down on his cot without removing his habit, throwing his tablet on the floor with such force, it cracked and broke. He lay there for a while, then rose up, and went to his little desk. He opened the drawer, took out some stationary that had been left there, and a pen, and he began to write. And he wrote until his hand began to cramp, from the effort, and then until the bells rang at 3:30 am, for Matins and Lauds.

Through the dark, Emerick stealthily followed Christoph. It brought him back to his military-training days, and this gave him a queasy feeling, as he darted along narrow, worn paths through woods and fields, with only the moon above as his light. He realized, once Christoph passed the site of the hermitage—now reduced to several stacked-up sheets of aluminum siding and torn apart wooden studs—where the novice was leading him. He watched as the boy peeled back a section of wire fencing at the monastery's perimeter, and headed into the state forest lands.

He continued to follow now through the midnight-dark woods, training his eyes on the tiny bobble of light Christoph carried, his bare feet encountering any number of barbs, sticks, rocks, large insects. He barely felt them, intent on tracking his quarry. Christoph stopped at last, in a spot unsettlingly close to where Lucian had been found dead. And then he turned, to face Emerick.

"You jerk! You shouldn't have followed me," said the boy, in a frightened way. "Marion said you would." He suddenly lurched toward Emerick. "Run! Get the hell out of here, I tell you that guy is frickin' *crazy*!"

Emerick realized that he had been lured and trapped. He turned around, to go back, but a flash of light hit his eyes: he ran headlong into Marion himself, carrying an electric lantern. The light illuminated Marion's pale, kind oval face, the inexpressible sadness in his eyes—all in a sickly, bluish light.

"Brother Emerick," Marion said, softly and sadly, as if he had caught him in a particularly sinful transgression. "What are you *doing* here? You're not in the army anymore. I fear you are suffering a most dangerous kind of delusion…"

"I'm not delusional, I'm perfectly sane. And I know you tricked me, into coming here. That only makes me think… My God, *you* killed Lucian, didn't you?"

"Emerick, he took his own life."

"Stop saying that!"

"I know, it's too painful to imagine or accept. How do you think we other monks feel about it? We mourn him as deeply as you do."

"Then what about the money in the hermitage, and the missing knot and---Don't come near me. I don't want you anywhere near—"

Emerick stepped backwards and suddenly a sharp root pierced his bare heel—the sudden pain of it causing him to lose his balance and fall completely backwards, onto the ground. And suddenly big Christoph was pinning him down against the ground by his shoulders, the lantern sitting beside their heads. Emerick stared into the novice's dilated, grayish-brownish eyes.

"I'm sorry, I'm sorry, Brother Emerick," Christoph whispered, desperately, as Emerick felt the horrifyingly familiar sensation of a needle pricking into his arm, the burning sensation of a substance being injected directly into his bloodstream---

"What—what is that? What did you give me?!" He began to fight and kick against both Christoph and Marion, while the infirmarian murmured soothing words to him—

"It's just a sedative, Brother, to calm you down. Ease your delusions. Stop fighting now, calm down, let the medicine do its work. We'll just leave you here for the night, let you rest, and meditate. Oh, you'll be safe here, no one comes out to these woods anymore. You'll be safe…"

Emerick tried to sit up, but suddenly felt the world spinning, a dark world punctuated with swirling sparks; his sight dimmed, as a heavy gray fog developed at the periphery of his vision, the lights from the lantern and flashlight strobing… Marion's and Christoph's voices came to him in random spurts, as if through a long tunnel:

….*can't … leave him…He's… He's…Go!*

And then he heard nothing more.

18.

Odo ran down to Matins and Lauds at 4:30 am. The lights had not yet been lit. But once they were, spilling across the small gathering of monks about the altar, his worst fears were confirmed. Marion, Isidore, and even Brother Christoph were there. The hem of

Christoph's robe was dotted with clinging burrs. He saw a few on Marion's robe as well. But no Emerick...

He was so upset, he jumped up and rushed from the chapel and into the night air, frantic. He looked wildly about, words forming, wild desperate prayers, in his brain. But then remembered Emerick's advice, to calm down and think clearly.

Emerick must still be in the forest. But where?

He ran inside, back down the corridor of the monastery's living quarters, to Emerick's room: The monks did not usually lock their doors, so he entered, and picked up from the floor the blue polo shirt that Emerick had recently worn into town. He pressed his nose into it and took a good, hard sniff: It was the very earthy, masculine essence of Emerick. Then he ran back outside with it.

He saw, coming up from the low road, a figure in pale, fluttering robes carrying a flashlight. Wearing a veil...

Maggy ran up to him. "Odo! Where's Emerick! He's not here, is he? Is he inside, at Vigil? I have to know!"

Odo shook his head.

"Oh, no! I just suddenly had this really bad feeling about him," She glanced wildly toward the woods. "Is he there, up there, Odo? Do you know?"

Odo grabbed her hand and led her first to the cider barn. There he knelt beside a sleeping Erdwulf and placed the shirt against his snout.

"Mmmer-rick," Odo said to the dog. "Find. Emm-rick."

The sleepy dog did not seem to understand at first, so Odo gently helped him up onto his feet, then pressed the shirt against his nose again. "Emerick!" he said a little more forcefully now, and then led the dog outdoors, where Maggy waited, puzzled.

"He's so old, Odo, plus I don't think sheepdogs can track—"

But as she spoke, Erdwulf suddenly began trotting up the hill in the dark. They followed him past the barn and orchard, past the torn-up hermitage, even to the spot in the fence where the wire was left gaping. Odo helped Maggy negotiate the tangle of metal and vegetation. Erdwulf led them into the state woods now, and Odo, stricken with fear and terror, nevertheless felt a growing sense of Emerick's nearness, like the warmth from a distant star...

19.

Emerick awoke, and it was still dark. But somehow, he was not in the forest anymore. He had the sense of being back at the chapel, feeling enveloped by a warm sort of darkness, Dark Vigil with the candles snuffed out. But no glowing image of native Mary and Jesus smiling down on him, only...that darkness.

He was still prone, on what seemed to be the chapel's stone floor, although he couldn't see it. Looking up, he saw only the tiniest pinprick of light far above, a single star. And somehow, he yearned for that star. He struggled to sit up, his body feeling stiff and strange and unwieldly. And then he saw a hand, reaching to him. A hand with long slender fingers, and the silver Celtic-braid ring of commitment that Lucian had worn.

"Come on, lad. Up with you now." Lucian smiled down at him, silver-haired and shining eyes and a big smile, wearing the pristine Philbertine habit he had *not* been buried in. No glasses, no cord about his waist... Emerick, gaping up at him, now grabbed handfuls of his robe to pull himself up, feeling the roughness of the raw cotton and linen in his fingers, and when he embraced Lucian, he felt the fullness of him, in his arms: Real, not an apparition, or hazy vision.

"Of course it's me! Who were you expecting, now. Go ahead, doubting Thomas: Inspect the wounds—" He pulled aside his cowl, and let Emerick slip his fingers into the crease of his neck, the faint pinkish streaks around his clavicle.

"You're not dead!"

154

"Ah, we don't use that word here, Emerick. Because *deadness* doesn't really exist, you know, life simply *is*. It goes on. In a different way…"

"Then…*I'm*…dead," Emerick whispered, but somehow this revelation did not disturb or horrify him. He felt only mild annoyance. "That maniac killed me! Before I had a chance to…" He gazed at Lucian—looking down a bit, because Lucian was, after all, half a head shorter than he. "Where are we, precisely?"

"Well, I think it's what you'd call in your own dialect, 'yonder.' It used to be known as limbo, or Purgatory. Not really what I expected, but definitely a kind of way-station, where sinners must wait, before we reach the Star." He glanced upwards, ruefully. "It's not so bad, really, rather like a perpetual Dark Vigil. Without the comfort of our Mother, or the other monks."

"Purgatory! Why you are you here, and not in…on the Star?"

"Ah Emerick. I know you think so well of me, as a good monk and paragon of virtue…I'm grateful for that, but no man is, especially myself. I'm here for a reason. I did not commit any kind of evil intentionally, but I let an evilness remain in the world, when I could have done something about it. A sin of omission, you might call it."

Emerick moved closer to him. "Who killed you? It was Marion, wasn't it?"

"You already knew everything you needed to know, to figure it out on your own, but somehow you never were able to hit on the solution."

"It's painful hearing you use the past tense for me. I don't think I'll ever get used to being dead. But please, go on."

"Let's have a sit-down. Look, here's a pew. Imagine, pews in Purgatory! Of course, no cushions on them…" He sighed and sat down and motioned for Emerick to join him. "Who do you think committed the dastardly deed, Emerick?"

"Well, Brother Marion of course. Because he just did the same thing to me."

"We don't know that you're dead yet, boyo. And he didn't wrap your cord around your neck, did he?"

Emerick looked down at his own waist, and saw his cord intact. "Wait. Are you tell me it *wasn't* Marion who killed you?"

Lucian smiled. "Just like any routine mystery story, the man—the monk--who killed me is the one you didn't necessarily suspect."

"Oh *no*. It's not Odo, is it? It *can't* be him, can it?"

"Of course it's not him, you dunce! You would have seen it in his mind, wouldn't you? But Odo does have his role in all this."

"Odrian?"

"No."

"Izzy?"

"Stop guessing and use your brain! Who did you say had a *true* motive, for killing me?"

Emerick stared at him for a long while, the answer slowly materializing:

"*Callixtus!*"

"He should have been your first—and only—real suspect."

"He was! In a way…when I ran into him at the hermitage that day, I thought for sure he had something to do with it. But, he's so affected and dramatic, I could never take him seriously…"

"That should have been your first clue. You don't think snipping a knot off his cord then sending it to my mistress is affected and dramatic? By the way, he still has *my* cord. I believe he's going about wearing it...."

Emerick gazed at Lucian's cordless waist. "I guess he *would* do something like that. But why would he kill you? Just so he could be head of the library? Because he did all that work on your book and you didn't give him any credit? That *was* kind of low of you."

156

"He didn't write it, I did! He would not have taken to violence for that, however. He just would have sulked and fumed, and then figured out someway to embarrass or discredit me."

"What made him *kill* you then?"

Lucian chuckled in a rueful way. "The next clue is where he left me. In the proverbial Heart-Break Forest."

"Where people hide out, and the druggies go to shoot up and folks commit suicide..."

"And where the heartbroken take refuge. Those destroyed by love..."

"Love! What's love got to do with it? Oh. Oh *no!*" Emerick put his head in his hands. "Please, please don't tell me...you and Callixtus were..."

"*I* had no interest in him, in that way. And even if I were of that orientation, I would never have chosen *him*, so high-strung and emotional and arrogant. But he developed a kind of erotic, neurotic fixation on me, from the moment he came to Holy Face. Surely you noticed, but you thought it was just his workstyle, that he was just being a good, and extremely attentive assistant. He was a top-notch translator, I must say. But always coming into the library, wanting to sit with me, talk with me. Walk with me. He never touched me, though, until that final day, when he put his hands around my neck—"

"Not the cord?"

"No, he added that later—that touch of drama, you know. But he snapped my neck like a twig. Strong boy, he was, and further fueled by madness, anger, humiliation. Inner demons."

" 'Course, you'd been drinking and taking pain pills too, so it wouldn't have taken much."

Lucian grinned, slyly, at him. "I told you, I was no saint!"

"But what made him snap like that? Just you rejecting him? Something you said?"

"Could be he saw dear old Mary, leaving the hermitage just as he was coming up, to say goodbye..."

"Ah! That's where she comes in. And I bet...She has something to do with a kind of drug scheme with Marion, Izzy, Odrian...Maybe she dropped off the money we found?"

"You're on the right track, lad. What her real motives were...I can't tell you. She was a most confounding sort of woman. But I did like her, quite a lot."

"Were you really planning to go off, and leave us? Never come back?"

"I had to, Emerick. The abbey had gotten itself into a terrible mess. A financial crisis, but also one of morals and ethics. I was partly to blame for that. I wanted to fix it somehow, bring the abbey back to what it was, when I first entered, but I didn't know how. So I decided to go back to the motherhouse for a long while and work on my own vows and commitment; and also discuss the situation frankly with the superiors there. I think what finally pushed me over the edge was when we got word that the Quebec monastery had closed, and the last monk was being sent to our abbey. A boy, just barely twenty, and I couldn't bear the thought...of another, young, hopeful monk coming to the cesspool our monastery had become. I had hoped the Order could somehow deal with it, or simply close the place. I'm not entirely sure Dom Frederique is up to challenge, although he seems a good man. Like the coward that I was, I chose to flee. But now I realize what the answer to the future is. Or, *who* the answer is." He paused.

"Odo?"

"No, the monk who has been persistently hunting for my killer these past several days—you must have a clue who that is!"

"But...but what can I do now? No one ever returns from the dead, do they?"

Lucian groaned, and slapped his head. "Have you *read* the New Testament?"

"Well, of course our Savior did, but...I don't know what I can do from here..."

"You're not *dead*, Emerick."

"You said I was."

"Ah, thick-headed as ever! I never said you were dead! I said you were experiencing a different type of *life*. Now, if Brother Marion explained it to you, he'd say you were having some kind of hallucinatory dream, made more vivid by the fact that the brain does, indeed, try to work out solutions to problems and dilemmas during sleep."

"So I'm just dreaming all this?"

"No. Not quite. This is a kind of reality, involving the sort of metaphysical belief we Catholics hold so dearly. Why is it you can understand Odo when he can't speak? Your sister is right, there is a divineness in that connection. You have already love, or charity, in your heart for fellow men; you have some modicum of hope still left; this, my boy, what you're experiencing now, is *faith*. You have the three big tools, to soldier on."

"But...how do I leave Purgatory? It's impossible, isn't it?"

"You are still connected to earth by the thinnest thread of life...You can go back whenever you like. Unless your heart suddenly starts fibrillating and stops. Let's hope that doesn't occur. That was a fairly lethal dose he gave you, you know, but you probably built up some kind of resistance or tolerance from your own time as an addict. Saved by your own past sins." He grinned. "You will live on, Emerick. And though the monastery will be badly damaged, humiliated and depleted of several monks, it will go on as well. You, and that little fellow from Quebec will be its redeemers, the instruments that bring it back into grace."

"No," Emerick told him sadly. "I don't think I can. I don't have the strength to go back there. I escaped death once before, in Afghanistan. Think this time it's got me for sure."

"Stop being obstinate and just do it! It's God's plan for you! Listen." He put a hand to his ear. "They're calling for you."

"I don't hear a thing."

"*Listen*, you fool!"

Emerick raised his head: And heard the faintest of calls, a soft, male voice calling him. *Emer-rick…Emer…rick….*"

"Is that…?"

"The voice, of the formerly voiceless…"

Erdwulf ran right up to the monk who was lying on the forest floor, just as dawn was beginning to break in the eastern sky. He licked at his battered, bloodied bare feet, then barked in an appreciative way.

Odo and Maggy ran up to Emerick, sinking down beside him. "Emerick!" Odo shouted, in relief and joy but also terror, too, because he could not tell if Emerick were alive. He was so still, barely breathing, and his face was dreadfully pale; one of his sleeves had been pushed up to reveal bruises and a dried-blood trail from the savage needle attack. Maggy took a cellphone she had wisely brought with her, and punched in 911. "Ambulance!" she shouted, "Stilton Mountain, the summit, Heart-break Forest! We're in the Heart-Break Forest, on the summit trail, south-west entrance, we've got an unconscious man here!"

Then she and Odo lay down and cradled themselves tightly around Emerick, wrapping the folds of their habits over him, trying to shield him from the faint, moist chill in the morning air. Maggy touched his cheek.

"Come on, little brother, wake up for us, come back to us, from wherever you went. And I know you went somewhere…Come on and open those sweet blue eyes, and let us know you're still with us."

"*Biff!*" Odo shouted one more time, close to his ear. And now Emerick's eyes fluttered open, staring up at the early morning sky through the trees, blankly turning to Odo, then Maggy…

"Where you been, boy?" she asked him, gently.

"Purgatory," he croaked. "But they done gone and kicked me out."

20.

While Emerick lay recovering, at Skerrittville General Hospital, life went on at Holy Face Monastery, though at a slowed and silent sort of pace. Marion and Christoph and even Isidore—the latter suffering a ferocious hangover—discreetly kept from sight, emerging only for meals and liturgy; while the others, such as Asaph, Brother Cook and Bart, sensing something amiss, whispered worriedly amongst themselves, as they tried to attend to their chores. Odo, when he returned with the abbot from the hospital in town, could not, of course, offer any verbal enlightenment, and the abbot remained stoically silent himself…until just before supper-time. He summoned Brother Cook in from the kitchen, as the other monks sat expectantly at the refectory table.

"Before we eat, I should tell you what has happened, with our Brother Emerick. He needs your prayers. He is in the town hospital, suffering the effect of a massive drug overdose. He was found early this morning in the state forest land. That is all we know."

"He's gone back to the drugs?!" Isidore showed true alarm.

"I am not making any judgement," the abbot said stiffly. "And neither should any of you."

"I should say," Marion spoke up. "I just want to put this out there…that some rather potent pain-killers and opiates have gone missing, from the infirmary—"

"You LIE!" Odo suddenly shouted. He pointed at Christoph, then at Marion. "You give drug to Emm-rick!"

Marion's expression did not change, but Isidore now turned to him. "You son of a b---- What the hell is wrong with you? Why would you give that boy drugs?"

"Allow me to explain. May I explain, abbot?"

"*Please.*"

"I did give him a mild sedative. He was distraught, after Chapter of Faults last night, I couldn't calm him down...I had no intention of killing him! You can't always predict how a drug is going to work with a particular person's metabolism."

"You drugged Emerick?" Callixtus, who had been silent until now, inexplicably started to chuckle. "Why didn't you do that sooner? Clearly he was in need of some kind of medication!"

There was a sudden silence, and then:

"Maybe you killed Lucian, too." This was the voice of old Bartolomeo, who directed a searing glance at Marion. The infirmarian quickly shook his head.

"I did not—and this is the absolute truth—have *anything* to do with the death of Father Lucian."

"Enough," the abbot said, wearily. "Marion, I will have much discussion with you later—privately. For now, let us eat. Then we will go to chapel, and pray, for the continuing recovery of our dear brother Emerick."

But as just as they were dismissed from supper—a gloomily silent meal of which no one could eat very much—Odo tugged on the abbot's sleeve, and handed him an envelope, bulging with what seemed a very long letter. Then he trotted off to Compline and what would be, as dusk fell on the abbey, his own night-long vigil for his fallen confrere.

162

In the morning, Emerick lay in his hospital bed, gazing at the sunshine pouring in through the window. An IV with hydrating fluid was still attached to his arm, but all in all, he felt almost normal again, and surprisingly calm. He felt a sense of quiet acceptance, the feeling that some hard truth had finally found a comfortable place in his brain.

Be still and know…Marion's drug had forced him, finally, into a near-fatal stillness. But through it, he had come to *know*.

The days before, after he'd been brought in by ambulance, had passed in a hazy, sleepy blur, with a choppy collage of visitors against the backdrop of the hissing oxygen tank, the stream of air hitting his compromised lungs. He seemed to recall brief visits with Maggy and Odo and his mother and grandmother, Gary and even old Bart from the monastery. And perhaps Ardelle the sheriff was by, too, but he could not remember what, if anything, he had said to her. In the middle of last night he woke, intermittently, from dreamless sleep, to hospital sounds of beeping call monitors and nurses padding down the hall; and he rejoiced, to still be part of the world.

Early that morning he was permitted a hot shower, and a big breakfast, which he wolfed down instantly, eggs and pancakes and biscuits and gravy and fruit salad, and now he lay back in his bed, clean, full, at peace. He recalled how he felt, when he first awoke on the forest floor, in the joint embrace of Odo and his sister and how comforting and good that was, after his return from 'yonder'—wherever that was.

And how good, how comforting to see Father Lucian again.

But there was still one matter, unresolved. How to bring Lucian's killer to justice…on the basis of what was either a near-death experience or true mystical vision, neither of which would be likely, he knew, to stand up in a court trial. Was Callixtus really the man who killed Lucian, or had he only imagined it?

163

Dr. Hilbert Wheeler walked in on his reverie, not in hospital scrubs or white jacket, but in a gray suit and tie, as if he had just been to church on a Sunday. He silently unhooked the IV line which had been delivering solution into Emerick's veins, then removed the port in Emerick's arm, covering the small wound with a bandage. He seemed faintly flushed, his mouth set in a grim line.

"You'll be leaving today," he told Emerick tersely. "I'd like to see you in a few days but...You were damned lucky. No heart problems, no more breathing difficulties, no brain damage. That was some dose you got. Maybe your previous experience with drugs helped. Or it may have made things worse. But you might have some withdrawal symptoms, over the next few days; won't be pleasant. Make sure the boys over there keep an eye on you."

"You look a mite preoccupied this morning, Doc."

Wheeler sank into the armchair by the bed. "Just came from the courthouse, the sheriff's office. Mary turned herself in this morning."

"Did she, now? For what?"

"I had no idea about her involvement in this drug-selling business, I just thought she was screwing around over there... Makes sense now, though. It was her way of digging at me, getting back at me. Of course, people think I'm involved, too; she knew that would happen. She wants to bring me down with her." He looked directly at Emerick. "You know this is going to get real ugly for the abbey, too, with the gang of four they're holding down there in custody as well."

"Not sure I understand...what you're referrin' to."

"Your compadres were selling drugs, in Heart-break Forest. Through a third party, of course. My wife was part of that; she was their high-society in-town connection. So, there's Father Odrian, Brother Christoph, Brother Isidore and the kingpin, Brother Marion, all in custody now. Your so-called overdose was part of their plan, I'm assuming, to keep you quiet and keep themselves going."

"But…how did that come out? I didn't even know…the full extent of it. I haven't spoken to anyone yet, I mean, anyone official…How did Ardelle know to go after them?"

"Your abbot turned them in."

"He did?"

"He did. He's out in the waiting area. You're good to go now. I'll sign you out. He can take you back with him."

Dom Frederique swept in, carrying a clean set of Emerick's robes on his arm. He looked as regal and proud as ever, his silver cross sparkling on his chest, but his voice was quiet, almost penitential.

"Are you ready to leave, Brother? I'll help you dress…"

Silently, he untied Emerick's hospital gown, and slid the white tunic over his head, helping him stand so he could pull it down straight. Then the scapular, the blue rectangular tabard that went over it, and finally the cord, which he simply handed to Emerick to tie on himself. Emerick felt both embarrassed and grateful for his help.

He sat back down on the bed, suddenly feeling a bit weak. He gazed at the one-knot cord in his hand, in a reflective way.

Dom Frederique stood before him, his hands clasped behind his back, his face a study in mourning.

"This is a very dark day, for Holy Face Monastery," he said, even as brilliant sun poured in from the window behind him. "Four of our monks, likely facing trial and prison. Our community reduced now, to only thirteen men. It is a great blow."

"How'd you find out about it all? The drug scandal, Marion attacking me?"

"Your young friend." Dom Frederique nodded. "He is an exceptional little monk. He let me know everything that was going on."

"*How?* Did he actually…*tell* you? Talk to you?"

"No. He wrote me a letter. An extraordinary letter. This is a photocopy—Mademoiselle Sheriff has the original. Evidence, you see. Which implicated Marion, Odrian, Isidore and unhappily, our new novice, Christoph, in a massive drug-selling scheme. A team of policemen came and scoured the monastery. They confiscated the big bag of money, which was in the cider barn. Another was found, in the medicine closet of the infirmary...as well as massive amounts of drugs and pills Brother Marion should not have had."

Emerick looked over the letter—it was several pages in length, in unexpectedly beautiful, graceful handwriting. And, entirely in French, which Emerick knew nothing of.

"His language is quite good, though he uses Canadian idioms and spellings. Apparently he tried, on his primitive toy computer, to record Brother Isidore's confession, but was unsuccessful. So he wrote down everything he could remember. It was a very difficult document to read. To think the monastery was supported, for years, by such an ugly business. That these monks preyed on the troubled people of this community. That they were planning to turn the monastery into a purely commercial venture! I shouldn't wonder that the town would want to see the abbey closed completely, never to open again."

"You'll find this is a very forgiving community," Emerick said softly. "Folks here are mostly poor, but rich in spirit. The monastery will go on, Abbot. Don't ask me how I know that, but I know."

"And five men lying, senseless, in the infirmary, likely Marion's victims as well."

"Ask Dr. Wheeler to come in and take a look. He might be able to help them."

"There is something still unclear." The abbot frowned. "Brother Odo's letter answers the question about the money. Lucian was apparently involved in the initial efforts to raise funds, but not with the drug selling. It also says, according to Brother Isidore, that Brother Marion might have been responsible for Lucian's death."

166

"Marion didn't kill Lucian," Emerick said, softly. "He might have been thinking about it, but I think another monk beat him to it."

"*What?* Not a fifth monk now, involved in all this?" Frederique turned ashen.

"I'm afraid so. But he wasn't involved in the drug-selling. Or maybe he knew of it, and said nothing. It didn't involve him. It was..." Emerick sighed, deeply. "A crime of *passion*."

"How do you *know* this? Did this monk confess to you?"

"No...and I'm not sure my charge would stand up in a court of law. You must believe me, Dom Frederique. Lucian told me in a ....well, a kind of vision, I reckon, while I was under. But once he said it, it all made sense to me."

"What sort of vision?"

"I didn't ask Doc Wheeler about it, but I think maybe...I might have actually *died* for a few minutes, and ended up in Purgatory. Where Father Lucian is now, waiting to go to Paradise."

The abbot looked at Emerick in a hard way, for a long time.

"Was it...Callixtus?"

Emerick nodded.

"Well then," the abbot said. "If that is the truth, we must hear it, from that monk's own lips."

"I doubt he'll ever admit to it, but it shocks me he can carry on, walking around the monastery as if nothing has happened."

"Even psychopaths can enter monasteries," the abbot said, with some sadness. "This matter could be very difficult to resolve. Otherwise, we may have to have Marion charged with the murder. He has already been charged with the attempt on your life."

"I can't believe...he tried to *kill* me."

"I fear now," the abbot said, slowly. "we will lose a sixth monk to this terrible scandal. After your experience...I should not be surprised if you decided..." He let the thought go unfinished.

"I don't know," Emerick said, quietly. "I can't get my head around how…all this was going on, while I was at the abbey, clueless, filling up with peace and strength, and growing closer to the Father, and…I don't know, I want more than anything to stay, but at the same time I feel…betrayed, like." He sighed. "And it's not over, it won't be over until…You're right, the murderer has to out himself. I have no real way to prove it. But I don't how to make him do that."

"All you need to do right now, is recuperate, get rest. Rest and pray, and the answer may come…" He glanced toward the door. "Yes, Brother Odo, you may come in now. We're ready to bring Emerick home."

Odo dashed in, looking quite trim in his newly made cotton-linen habit, which Maggy had sewn up expertly: it fitted him perfectly, unlike the clumsy oversized wool habit he had been wearing.

"Hey!" Emerick exclaimed, at the sight of him. "Lookin' sharp, pal!"

Beneath the hem of Odo's tunic peeked the oversized bright-red plastic thongs Emerick had given him, which *thwapped* against the hospital linoleum; he in turn handed Emerick a brown paper bag, which contained his grandmother's blue-rose flip-flops. Emerick grinned when he saw them and slipped them on immediately.

"Yeah, won't be going barefoot for awhile, not till the bottom of my foot heals. I should probably get some of those official monk sandals."

Odo also handed Emerick a bright gold-orange apple, one of the fully ripened summer apples, with a single leaf still attached to it.

Emerick gazed at it.

"This your way of telling me, we got work to do?"

Odo nodded.

He rose, and walked toward the door, with the abbot's hand on his back, and Odo right alongside him. "We still have a *lot* of work to do, I guess," he said, sadly, "if we're gonna save the abbey."

21.

Dom Frederique began that night's meeting.

"Yes, I know it is unusual to have *two* Chapters of Faults in one week, but apparently the last one was not so successful, or truthful, as you all understand now. We have one monk dead, another recovering from a pharmaceutical attack, and four brothers in police custody, and what I need to know, if I am to continue keeping this abbey open, is if anyone else has anything more to confess…anything that might, for example, be against the laws of this country."

He was met with stunned silence. Meanwhile, Emerick was making his way into the refectory and took a seat at the table, looking mildly fatigued but otherwise healthy. He took care to sit some distance from Brother Callixtus.

"It was Brother Infirmarian who gave Emerick the poison, no?" Brother Cook asked. "I am hoping you don't think it is my cooking."

Emerick laughed. "No, Chef. But I would like to give you a few suggestions, when all this is over with."

"I'm sorry, Emerick," said Callixtus now, in a soft voice. "That could not have been a pleasant experience for you. You've emerged as quite the hero in all this, uncovering the abbey drug ring. Lucian, I should think, would be quite proud of you."

Emerick made no reply. He stared down at the table. Odo, meanwhile, sitting beside him, stared up the table at Callixtus in horror, having just realized the conclusion Emerick had come to about Lucian's murder.

The abbot cocked his head, in a faintly suspicious way. "You had no knowledge of this activity, Brother Callixtus? You've been known to visit the hermitage now and then."

Callixtus seemed startled. "I had nothing to do with that criminal endeavor, Dom Frederique."

"We know you didn't," Emerick said, in a bland way. "But hanging out at the hermitage like you did, you must have *heard* something. I mean, Lucian knew all about it, apparently…and you were real close to Lucian, weren't you? Closer to him than I was…"

"We never discussed it." Callixtus said, stiffly.

"Did you know Lucian wasn't planning to come back from France?" Emerick asked.

Callixtus waited a while before answering. "Yes."

"Did you know why?" the abbot now asked.

"He…He couldn't be here anymore. That's what he told me. I had assumed…he was having a crisis of faith. But I know now, it was because of the drug selling. He would not have wanted to be part of that."

"You met with him, the night he died, didn't you?" said Emerick. "At the hermitage?"

"I did. As you say, I knew he wasn't coming back."

"You guys had some kind of argument? A fight?"

"No. Are you the district attorney now? Cross-examining me? I'm sorry Marion almost killed you, but why are you still conducting this witch hunt?"

"Because we haven't gotten to the truth yet. What *happened* between you two that last night?"

"I don't have to tell you that, it was between myself and Father Lucian."

"Okay, let me tell you then." Emerick sat up straight. "Let me tell you about Father Lucian's last night on earth. See if I got it right, Clix, because it's all just a theory, right now. Father Lucian asked you specifically to meet him at the hermitage, the night he died, isn't that so?"

"Yes, to say good-bye, I assumed...Give me final instructions, regarding his book, running the library..."

"But you felt a little differently about Lucian than the rest of us did."

"I believe that's true," Calixtus said, slowly. "I don't think any other monk had the kind of regard and respect I had for Lucian. Except, perhaps, for *you*, Emerick."

"Your love for Father Lucian was of a completely different nature than mine."

Callixtus' dark-gray eyes bored into him. "Are you implying that we had an *improper* relationship?"

"No, that's the thing. I don't think you had *any* kind of relationship with him. Chaste or unchaste. But you wanted to. It drove you crazy, to see him so chummy with *me*. And the other monks. But not you, his own assistant. He was always a mite... *cold* to you, wasn't he? And yet you'd go and do anything he asked. I know you were doing most of the work on that St. Philbert project. And I know, Father Lucian wasn't the perfectly holy and moral man I believed him to be. You saw that too, the darkness, the weakness, but you wanted to jump right into it. You thought, if he can be immoral and unchaste with others, why can't he be like that...with *me*?"

The other monks, and the abbot as well, sat riveted, watching Callixtus' expression. He seemed faintly stunned.

"I...believe that drug overdose you endured must have affected your thinking processes, Brother Emerick. You are positively *delusional*."

"And so, when you hiked up that ol' hill toward the hermitage," Emerick continued, ignoring him, "and saw his secret sweetheart, Missus Weatherspoon coming down, you—" He snapped his own fingers. " 'Cause you knew she had the kind of relationship, that you really wanted with Lucian, but he wouldn't ever let you have."

Callixtus sat back now, regarding Emerick with cool amusement.

"That's quite the imagination you've developed, farm boy. Maybe that drug did you some good."

"Continue, Brother Emerick," the abbot said, in a stony voice. The other monks leaned forward to catch Emerick's every word.

"It's not out of my imagination, and it's not a story I would ever want to tell," Emerick continued. "Because when you got to the hermitage, you began to act in a very untoward way toward Lucian. Maybe you'd been drinking some of that expensive wine beforehand." Emerick shook his head regretfully. "It must have right *humiliating*, when Lucian rejected you outright, like that."

"Never happened."

"Maybe you quarreled. Maybe Lucian read you the riot act. I don't know exactly what happened in those last few minutes, but somehow his life was snuffed out, just like that."

"And how does he end up in the middle of what you call Heartbreak Forest?"

"You tell me, Clix."

"This is an utterly ridiculous, *disgusting*, story, Emerick, I can't believe even *you* would be low enough to tell it. Do you really hate me that much? Your fellow brother?"

Emerick rose now and slowly advanced toward Callixtus.

"Are you going to attack me again?" Callixtus taunted.

"No." He stood right in front of him. "I want you to tell me to my face, that you had nothing to do with Lucian's death. Look me in the eye and say it."

"Sit down, Emerick. You look seriously fatigued."

"Not until you tell me, and every other monk at this table. The truth."

"Why are you *doing* this?" Callixtus now looked pained. "Haven't the brothers been through enough? Why do you continue with this?"

"Because I *have* to."

"Why do you think *I'm* the killer?"

"Lucian told me so."

There was a long moment of silence around the table. Callixtus looked frozen in shock for a moment, then dissolved into chuckling, folding his arms together.

"And when did he tell you this? Before, or after, he died?"

"I saw him, when I was laid out in the woods, I saw him and talked with him, and he told me, you killed him. He told me how, and why."

Brother Cook, the mystic, made the sign of the cross on himself. But Callixtus merely shook his head.

"Dear God," he murmured. "You've gone completely insane. What in the name of Satan did Marion inject into you?"

"You might as well confess, because there ain't no death sentence anymore in West Virginia. But you'll probably get life. Kind of ironic, that use of words there, isn't it."

"Dom Frederique, please, can you put an end to this nonsense?"

"I have *proof*, Clix." Emerick said, suddenly.

"Proof, of some non-existent vision? I'd like to see that!"

Now Emerick moved to the sitting Callixtus, bending over and seeming to embrace him. But when he returned to standing, he was holding the monk's cord in his hand. He showed it to the others, as if it were an ancient and holy relic.

"This is Father Lucian's cord. It was Brother Callixtus' cord that was found with his body, in the forest."

The other brothers gasped. "But...it's only got one knot!" said Brother Bart.

"Yes, Clix clipped off the priestly knots." Emerick held up one end. "And fairly recently, too, because it hasn't frayed yet. Can't believe we didn't notice it sooner."

"It's not Lucian's cord," said Callixtus in an incredulous voice. "It's *mine*. Our cords are identical, all of them."

"Except they're *not*. Look, it's the old style, made of cotton and hemp, and the knots are tied a little differently. You entered the year before I did," he said, to Callixtus, "when they switched over to the acrylic-polyester blend. See—" He compared the cord to his own, which was a bit brighter and smoother. "These new ones are stain-proof. And see these stains on Lucian's cord?" He put it front of Callixtus' face. "You're so fastidious, how could you even wear a dirty ol' cord with these big stains on it. Can you explain those?"

"They're not... they're not blood, if that's what you're implying." But Callixtus, indeed, finally seemed rattled.

"No, they're not. Not wine, neither, your drink. They're this kind of greenish color. You know what that is, don't you?"

"I suppose you'll tell me."

"*Philbertine!*" Odo shouted, almost in delight, from the other end of the table.

"It's the herb liqueur he and Izzy were working on together. And don't tell me you were drinking that stuff on a regular basis!"

The monks murmured, and nodded their heads. Brother Bart slapped the side of his face. "Well, I'll be darned! Just like in the movies!"

Callixtus stared at Emerick for a long time, then stood up. "This is *absurd*. If you're finished playing amateur detective, I have other matters to attend to. Might I be excused now, Abbot?"

"I think not, Brother," said the abbot, sternly. "I think you must talk to Mademoiselle Sheriff, and let her interview you about Father Lucian."

"I have no reason to do so, Dom Frederique. If I'm not *guilty*, of any crime," said Callixtus calmly. "This is not an official court of law, is it?" He bowed low to the abbot before leaving the refectory, heading in the direction of the library.

Emerick turned to the abbot. "What...what do we do now? Call Ardelle anyway?"

Dom Frederique shook his head sadly. "We will. But not just yet: Let us give him time to absorb this, resolve his conscience. We will all pray for him, in the meantime. But also, keep the eye on him. In the morning, I personally will take him to the sheriff...." He rose. "Go and rest now, Emerick. You need not rise for Matins tonight, we will see you at Mass in the morning. In the light of day, we can only hope, all things will become visible."

For some time after Compline that night, Odo stood outside the door to Emerick's room, literally standing guard. He feared, somehow, that Callixtus might come and harm Emerick, after the confrontation in the refectory. He did not know if he could physically fight off Callixtus, but hoped his mere presence there might keep him away. And it seemed to work...until the abbot himself came, and gently shooed Odo back to his own room.

"You need your rest, too, little brother. You have already shown us, how very valuable you are, a true treasure to this poor abbey. You could not have come at a better time."

Emerick, meanwhile, tossed and turned on his hard, narrow bed, already missing the rather more plush—and adjustable—mattress from the hospital. Way past midnight, it was still as hot and humid as mid-day, and beads of sweat formed on his bare chest, as he tried to think cooling thoughts, and prayed for just a bit of a breeze to come through his wide-open window.

But deep into the night, just after the bell sounded for Matins, hour of souls, he heard his doorknob rattle a bit. He tensed—for he had taken the precaution of locking it, fearing an unwanted visit in the middle of the night, in possible retaliation for the last Chapter of Faults.

Then came the knock—soft, almost penitential. Now Emerick rose, a little sleepy now and wearing only striped boxer shorts. He cracked the door open.

Callixtus stood on the other side. No longer in monk's habit, but in ordinary men's clothes, shirt and slacks, but monk's sandals still on his feet. A small suitcase sat nearby.

"Emerick, let me in a moment. I need to talk to you." His voice was terse, urgent.

"Whatever you gotta say, say it here."

"It's not the kind of discussion I want to have in the hallway."

"The others are at Matins. What do you care?"

"Emerick, I'm not here to hurt you, can we just…talk, like rational adults? Like ordinary men? I want to make peace with you, I'm going away, I'm leaving, but I have something to ask you."

Reluctantly, Emerick stepped aside, and let him enter. He went and sat down on the bed because he was, truth to be told, feeling a little queasy now.

"What did you want to ask me, Clix? About my time with Father Lucian, the other night? I'm not sharing any more of that with you."

"I'm no longer Callixtus anymore. Just Timothy. Tim."

"What do you want?"

"Emerick. I want you to come with me. Will you come with me, away from this place?"

"*What?*"

"Yes, it's shocking, isn't it? We've always been…rivals, of a sort. Oil and water. Two brothers, getting on each others' nerves. Being a scholar, I can't help but reference the old apocryphal story of the Archangels. But somehow I was cast into the role of Lucifer, and you the golden shining warrior Michael. Two brother angels, competing for the attention of the wise but imperfect god. But that god is dead, so…there is no reason, for either of us to be here anymore."

"Now who's delusional?" Emerick muttered. "I'm not going any-freaking-where with you."

"What's left here for you? The abbey is in financial ruin. Mired in scandal. There are only a handful of monks left. You're not even

176

thirty yet. What do you think you will do, with the rest of your life? Leave here now, and get a head start, on the future."

"A future...with *you*?"

"You say that like it's a bad thing!" Callixtus laughed. "We can shed this tiresome dogma, this fictional construct of the Church and the so-called sanctity of the monastery. We will embrace the world, embrace its pleasures, as two enlightened, fully alive men! There is no afterlife, our only Heaven awaits beyond the monastery gate!" He took a step closer to Emerick. "I know you've had doubts all along, no doubt fostered by your dreadful experiences in Afghanistan. Admit it, you've been thinking of leaving all along, and even more so now, after this last debacle." He edged a little closer. "Can you honestly tell me, you've never had the desire to chuck the habit, just leave, just start walking and not look back? Can you?"

"I'm not discussing my doubts with you," Emerick whispered, drawing back. "I might have them, but not once, not even in the hospital, did I ever *not* want to come back here—"

"Listen to your doubts. That's your own brain and reason, working through the mucky fiction of faith."

Emerick suddenly put his hand to his head. "It's not real, it's not happening...I'm not really talkin' to you right now, I'm hallucinatin', only imaginin', what I think you would do...Must be some kind of dream or vision—" Suddenly he was knocked backwards onto his butt by a sharp blow to his upper chest, the sound of Callixtus' laughter in the background: "Did *that* feel like a dream or a vision?"

Emerick's hands instantly coiled themselves into fists, but somehow he kept them still, slowly rising back to his feet.

"Wake up, farm-boy! This is reality, this is no dream. Come with me, make the most of your life. We could be very good together. Opposites attract, you know." He then reached to help Emerick with the utmost delicacy, the way a lover might reach out to a beloved. Emerick recoiled, his hands still tightly balled fists.

"What's *wrong* with you?" he murmured to Callixtus. "Can't you relate to people in any other way?"

"Oh, come on. Biff. You've spent your adult life surrounding yourself with men: First the army, and then the monastery. I don't think you actually *know* yourself. You only say you like girls because you think you're supposed to. You might be surprised, at your capacity to love in a different way—"

And now suddenly Emerick saw a flash of white, and released his right fist, sending it flying squarely into Callixtus' jaw, knocking him over. He regretted the punch almost instantly, stunned at how quickly it had come upon him, how his fist had flown into action before he could even think about it.

And Callixtus, sitting on the floor and rubbing his jaw, could only laugh.

"Hit a nerve, did I? Maybe your doubts extend beyond the spiritual..."

Emerick rubbed his stinging knuckles. "Shouldn't have hit you...happened before I could stop it..."

"You see, how much alike we are. How quick to anger, and react, without thinking," said Callixtus, as he rose to his feet. "Maybe you understand me better now, since you're full of such raw emotion yourself. Maybe now you understand that primitive need to strike out, to be violent without thought or reason. It's in all of us, my boy, and no amount of monkhood and contemplation can leech it out of us."

"Just tell me, before you go," Emerick said, softly, still rubbing his fist. "I need to hear you say it."

"What? What am I supposed to say?"

"You know. I need to hear you admit it."

"Admit what?" Callixtus seemed to be playing with him, teasing, his voice almost merry.

Emerick grew closer to him, so close their faces were almost touching. "Admit to me, that you killed Father Lucian." He stared into Callixtus' eyes, dull dead gray in that darkened room, with only a sliver of moon outside, those eyes were all he could see, and there was no hardness in them, no anger, but also no regret, no sorrow, so sign of conscience. Emerick struggled not to look away, waiting for the answer he wanted to hear. Callixtus gazed back at him for long moment.

"It was... an accident," he murmured.

"You accidentally strangled him to death."

"If you're going to get snide—"

"Just go on."

"You were freakishly... right. I don't know how you got the details but..." He whirled around, and began pacing. "I went up to the hermitage, as he asked me to. There was fat old Mary, waddling back down the hill. God, what did he see in that cow? The mother thing I guess...And there he was, in bed, *after*...and already out of it, two sheets to the wind as they say, and who knows how many pain-killers he took. You were right. He could sin with her, but not me. I had to punish him. I wanted him to wake up...in sheer *terror*. Just to shake him up, wake him up mentally...He was living a lie, Emerick! Preaching the glories of monastic life, living like a sinful fool. Do you think that's right?"

"We're all of us sinners, Brother."

"Oh, shut up."

"You used your hands, and then the cord."

Callixtus fell silent.

"You used your hands, but then the cord, after he was already dead. Because you'd already thought up the suicide angle."

"How can you possibly know this?" Callixtus whispered. "It was only a matter of *seconds*. I don't even think a full minute went by. Before I knew it, he was dead."

"He was already compromised by the alcohol and the opiates. Believe me, I know what them things can do."

"I didn't expect he would be found in the woods right away. I figured some winter day, someone would stumble over his skeleton."

"But you hung the rope over the tree, and kicked over the stump, just for insurance."

"If that mute twit from Quebec had never stumbled into the woods that day…Life would be going on as usual, here at the monastery, no revelations about money or drug-selling, and you'd be out there just picking apples. And there's the gist of it, Ricky. The abbey is ruined, and it's *all your doing*. Didn't you have any idea what this would all lead to?"

For a long while, Emerick did not answer, his mind feeling caught in a fuzzy, hazy web, struggling with this new story which now cast him as a villain. But suddenly, a thin shaft of light seemed to flood into his brain, and it was the same sort of light he *felt*, shining down on him in Purgatory.

"The abbey will continue, Lucian told me so. And I believe that. But I don't know what'll become of you, Callixtus. You can leave the monastery and pretend it never existed, but how can you live with this truth, this black… *knowledge* in your brain? There is still some good left in you, I know there is. Turn yourself in, repent, and maybe there's hope…"

But Callixtus only laughed in a callous way, and rose to his feet. "Your piety, your earnestness, is so appealing, Emerick. Combined with those blue eyes of yours, almost irresistible. But also pathetic and ridiculous." His words were filled with bravado, but Emerick heard the slight quaver, the undertone of uncertainty and bitterness and despair. "Okay, you can rot here. I'm moving on, to a better life. An afterlife, you might say…" He turned to go.

"Go ahead and leave." Emerick snapped. "I'll give you a one-minute head start. One minute, and then I'm calling the sheriff on you. They'll catch you before you even get to the bottom of Stilton Mountain."

"Then give me two minutes," Callixtus replied, archly, before slipping out of Emerick's room.

As soon as he left, Emerick jumped up and grabbed his habit, pulling Izzy's cellphone from his pocket, only to find the battery completely dead. He threw the phone onto the floor, and sank down onto his bed, overcome with a powerful wave of fatigue, squeezing his brain, filling it with an urge to sleep. He slumped back down onto his cot, his shoulder still smarting sharply from where Callixtus had hit him, and fell into a stupor-like sleep.

In the morning, two more monks were missing from the daily Mass. The abbot, seeing the fright on Odo's face, went to him at once.

"Callixtus has likely fled. But Emerick is surely still sleeping off the effects of his drugging. We won't disturb him."

But Odo fidgeted during the entire liturgy, repeatedly turning toward the door, as if he expected Emerick to arrive at any time. At the end of Mass, and before breakfast, the abbot himself escorted Odo to the dormitory. They stopped first at Callixtus' room, first cracking, then fully opening the door. No one was inside, and his habit lay spread neatly on the bed.

They moved on to Emerick's room, and found the door unlocked. But they already heard him snoring. Peeking in, they saw him lying deep in slumber, diagonally across his bed, flat on his stomach, in his striped boxers, his pale hair well-tussled. Odo immediately went in and grabbed his arm to wake him, but the abbot tried to pulled him back.

"Let him sleep," he scolded, but Emerick began to move, groaning slightly. He turned a little toward the abbot and Odo, then started.

"Yikes! Why'd you let me sleep so long?"

"You were in need of it," The abbot intoned.

"I guess. What a night." He rubbed his face. "What...a *crazy* dream I had. I reckon it was a dream, or vision, it was like that thing with Lucian, except Clix was in it—"

"Callixtus is gone."

Emerick blinked several times. "Yeah, he told me that...in my dream..." He rolled over and sat up. And now Odo, gasping, reached out and pointed to the deep half-moon blue-black bruise on his chest, near his shoulder. Emerick, too, noted it with some surprise, and a bit of horror.

"How did you get that, Brother?" the abbot asked, startled. "I didn't see it the other day, in the hospital."

Emerick again looked down, at the spot where the heel of Callixtus' hand had met his chest. "He *was* here," he said, softly. "Left his mark on me. But I left one on him too." He looked up at the abbot, in a bewildered way. "Now he's gone..."

"I will contact Mademoiselle Sheriff at once. They will perhaps find him."

"Maybe," Emerick murmured, in an uncertain way. "I do hate the idea, of someone like him being out in the world."

22.

A week passed since Brother Callixtus' disappearance, and then another. Three of the four monks taken from Holy Face Monastery continued to be held in custody, awaiting trials for various degrees of attempted murder, theft, and illegal drug possession. No money was raised for their bail, and the abbot formally expelled the three from the monastery. Only Brother Christoph was not charged—at Emerick's behest—and let go, into the custody of the abbot himself, who brought him back to finish his novitiate; he seemed relieved to be back, and promised to follow the instructions of the drug counselor overseeing his de-toxification program. He was sorely needed at the infirmary, where five infirm monks still remained and which lacked immediate supervision with Marion deep in legal trouble.

With so few able-bodied monks left, all hands on deck were needed for harvest season. But Brother Emerick had apparently not yet recovered yet from his own ordeal. He was unnaturally silent, unsmiling, causing both Odo and the abbot grave concern. He worked, in a mechanical way, with Odo and Asaph and even the abbot himself, picking and storing the summer-ripening apples in big crates and baskets in the barn, although the future of the abbey's famed hard cider was definitely in question. Emerick said he could not remember the fermenting formula, and it could not be found in Brother Isidore's profoundly messy office.

After they had spent their working day in the orchard, Emerick did not join the others in the chapel or even for supper, but instead would wander out to the Heart-break Forest. Here he would walk and comb the woods for hours, walking barefoot along its trails, searching for who knew what. Odo would watch him go, mournfully, wanting to go after him, but knowing this was something Emerick somehow had to do, to help himself recover completely. The abbot, too, took notice of this, and discussed with the remaining monks whether a therapist from town might need to be brought in. The consensus was that Emerick be given a few more weeks, before outside reinforcements were called in.

But after two weeks or so, Odo decided to take action on his own. He knew this action would require him to *speak* to Emerick, perhaps at length, and so, for days beforehand, he practiced and rehearsed the words he would say, trying to make himself sound natural and unforced, hoping to convey, somehow, in his voice, the sympathy and worry and concern he felt inside.

He waited one evening, when Emerick had already been gone a few hours, and had missed Compline. He made his way to the forest, with a flashlight, and Erdwulf by his side, and eventually they located Emerick on a distant path in the woods, just as the sun had set. It was September now, and there was a new coolness in the air, even a slight hint of winter.

Emerick looked up in surprise at Odo and the dog, but did not greet them. Odo stepped forward. "Emerick," he said, in a steady voice. "You must come home now. *Si vous plait.*"

Emerick nodded.

"You have labors...work."

"I know," Emerick said, softly.

"Not only *les pommes*. We must...bury Father Lucian, again. Bring him back on to, errr, *in to*, abbey ground."

At this Emerick's mouth fell open a little. "Are you...are you *talking*, now, Odo?" He smiled now. "Are you? 'cause that's what I need. I *need* you to talk to me. And *I* need to talk, that mind meld thing is okay, but I really, really need...to just talk *with* you. Back and forth, like."

Odo nodded eagerly. "I am..." He struggled for the right idiom. "Working on it. At it. It is hard for me. But I can do it. In English, I am hoping."

"I hope so too, 'cause I don't know a word of French Canadian." He grinned at Odo and even laughed a little, a kind of chuckle that combined relief and ruefulness. He began to walk alongside Odo and Erdie, back toward the edge of the woods. "I've just been...I didn't mean to ignore you and the others. I just had to come out here. At first, it was to look for, you know, *him*..."

"Father Lucian?"

"No. I know where he is. I was looking for Callixtus." Emerick gazed up, in a pained way, up around the trees. "I just thought...I was convinced, he would be out here, hiding out. I was thinking, he

184

wanted to be caught out. Caught out and punished. But that was my own delusion. After awhile, I just started looking for his corpse, because I thought that might be more likely... I thought, he could be buried in the hole we had Father Lucian in. They haven't found Clix yet, have they, the police?"

"I do not know. I do not think so."

"Maybe he's here, maybe not. But life has to go on. The living have to keep living. You see, all this walking, in the woods...it's helped me. It's helped me tremendously. I learned...that you can be still, while moving. You can keep walking, but your mind can slow down and grow calm, and then the good thoughts come. I've been thinking about all those poor people in Skerritville, stuck on drugs. I've been thinking of troubled people, everywhere. And I was thinking, maybe we could make amends somehow, by setting up a retreat house like other monasteries have, a kind of hermitage—but for anybody who needs it. The original Philbertines, they were hostellers, they took travelers in. We could go back to that, not just be off by ourselves here. I have to talk to the abbot about it, I don't know how it would work..."

"But the apples?" Odo asked, in an uncertain way.

"That should still be our main work. We'll always make cider, no matter what. You know, when I was out there, I remembered the fermenting formula! Nothin' to it. I could talk to Maud, down in town, and see if she can send some kids up to help with the rest of the harvesting. There's gonna be tons of those Winesaps in October!"

They paused at the edge of the orchard now, looking down on the monastery cloaked in dusk, its chapel window still lit up and glowing in stained-glass colors.

"Yes, I think I'm going to be here, for quite a long while to come," said Emerick, with a quiet certainty in his voice.

185

But Odo, standing beside him, said nothing, gazing down at the abbey with an expression that suddenly seemed tinged with vague uncertainty.

After a while, the two young monks walked downhill together toward the monastery proper, as the ancient sheepdog Erdwulf trotted loyally at their side.

Finis

Coming up Next:
NAMES OF THE FATHERS

Barefoot Monk Mystery #2: Join Brothers Emerick and Odo as they explore more personal terrain: Odo struggles to unravel the mystery of his own birth and background, a quest that unintentionally throws his vocation into doubt; while Emerick struggles with a dying father's revelation, and the arrival of a mysterious fellow monk from Europe.

For more information, visit www.kpcecala.net

Made in the USA
Lexington, KY
28 February 2019